Praise for NORMAL CURVE?

Normal Curve? tener duende.

There is something really special about the word duende. It has a Spanish origin and is used to describe art through the phrase tener duende (to have duende) or to have the quality of evoking overwhelming emotion through expression. And while it was originally only used to describe a flamenco dance performance that was so moving to the audience, it is now also used to describe songs, movies, literature, or any form of art that evokes the same "feel it in your chest" type of influence when taking it in.

What I think is particularly special about this word is that it serves as a reminder of how art connects us at the heart. Whether it's two people listening to a song and look into each other's eyes as the melody moves them together, or a single person admiring a painting and feeling the weight of emotion the artist put into the piece, it's a sense of connection that adds so much richness and beauty to Life.

To be able to experience something that has duende is both a privilege and a mindset. We must open our eyes and hearts in order to enjoy these little moments of magic. It is a hand-hold, a connection of empathy and understanding that says "I'm here with you," and what a powerful expression of love that is.

Normal Curve? is duende.

I am so honored to read *Normal Curve?* before it's officially out. I wanted to recap why I loved the book so much. Probably most of all, I love the emotional intelligence, rawness of and managing complex feelings by men—I think we are lucky to be surrounded by men like this (either being from liberal cities, being around queer folks or just now being in 2024) but I genuinely hope that more straight (& not! It's not exclusively them ha ha) men can read this and just think about how much richer our relationships could be if we break down the patriarchal/toxic masculinity walls and open our hearts to love, understanding & empathy.

All in all, my heart was glowing the entire time I read this.

—Dr. Camille Cardenas, PT, DPT

Busterfly

a small, personal, fun-loving publishing company

Also by Stephen J. Mulrooney in the *NORMAL?* Series
NORMAL?
NORMAL TOO?
(Yes, you should read these first.)

NORMAL CURVE?

STEPHEN J. MULROONEY

Busterfly
Kansas City, Missouri

Busterfly

Kansas City, Missouri

First Busterfly edition 2024

Busterfly and Busterfly logo are trademarks of Busterfly LLC

Printed in the United States of America

ISBN: 978-1-966476-00-9 (Paperback)
978-1-966476-01-6 (eBook)

Dedication

NORMAL CURVE?, like *NORMAL?* and *NORMAL TOO?*, the books that preceded it, is dedicated to the man who has made everything wonderful in my life possible, my husband and publisher, Jerome P. Van Wert.

Jerome has encouraged and inspired me to write for the forty-two years we've been together. And although it took about thirty of those years for the resolve to finally kick in, he never gave up on me. It was Jerome who finally gave me the courage to sit down and write. And it was Jerome who ultimately gave me the courage to call myself an author and continue writing.

As the publisher of my books, every page of every story passes carefully through his loving hands before going to print. He designs the covers, chooses the artists and editors, and picks the best book designer. He protects and carefully guides them through the dozens of steps of the publishing process until he is satisfied that the books are beautiful works of art.

Although he refuses to take credit for them, because of his constant dedication to and nurturing of them, they are our books. They couldn't possibly be in better hands—and they would never have reached your hands without him.

Like the old song made popular by The Shirelles, and written by Lowman Pauling and Ralph Bass, constantly exclaims, "This is dedicated to the one I love."

Acknowledgements

There are so many people to thank for their assistance in bringing this book to light. Their input and expertise have been invaluable, and I am sure that you will find their hard work has helped transform this story into a beautiful work of art.

First, and foremost, I want to thank my publisher, Busterfly, and in particular, Jerome Van Wert, for his expertise in editing and publishing this book, and for his careful selection of the many talented hands it passed through before reaching yours.

Our main editor, Elizabeth Anderson is such an extremely talented individual that I can't imagine publishing a book without first passing it through her professional hands. If you find any punctuation throughout the text that you don't agree with, it is because it has been added for emphasis, and not because it has escaped her watchful eye.

I would also like to thank Madeleine Hogan, John and Sandra Hudson, Clara Keller, Andrew Appel, and Dr. Camille Cardenas for their editing skills, reviews, and recommendations.

Finally, no book is complete without a great book design. A great book design requires a great book designer. I am fortunate to have the best, Clark Kenyon at Camp Pope Publishing.

Andrew Batcheller

We would like to particularly make a special acknowledgement of our dear friend and incredible artist, Andrew Batcheller. Upon reading the first two books in this *Normal?* series, he was so moved by their content, Andrew asked us if we would allow him to paint the cover of the next book in the series, *Normal Curve?,* and accept it as a gift to us. We were overwhelmed by the offer from such a great artist. It was with the most heart-based gratitude that we accepted. That painting is now reproduced as the cover art of this book.

Andrew Batcheller, a Kansas City native who has called Joplin, Missouri, his home for the last decade, classifies his work as "portraiture" using birds as analogies for the human condition. The emotional quality of his work evokes thoughtful contemplation of our own human drama. His award-winning paintings are a part of national and international collections, and to our great fortune, a reproduction of one of his paintings graces the cover of this book, *Normal Curve?.*

To view other works by Andrew Batcheller, go to

www.andrewbatcheller.com

Prologue

Mother once told me, "Every life is a series of stories, and most lives are hundreds of stories tall. It's impossible to read them all, and it's often difficult to distinguish between the fiction and the non-fiction chapters in each one. So, the only way to get to really know someone is through the Reader's Digest version, one issue at a time."

Whether or not you take Mother's guidance literally, or find some issue with the issue, it is important to remember that Mother's also the person who told me, "Never use the expression, 'Keep your shirt on,' when talking to a good-looking guy." So, there's much to be said for how learned his learned advice is.

The point is, there are hundreds of stories behind the story I'm about to tell you, and every character is an anthology unto themselves. If you have followed their stories before, you are aware of their back issues. If not, I trust that there is enough of the Reader's Digest version that follows to give you enough gist for the mill.

This is a story so real, and yet so magical, that you might well think it's fiction. But only those who don't believe in magic will find it so. For the rest of us, the only difference between a literary life, and a physical life, is that a literary life lasts forever.

My name is Gene Poole-Hall. Hopefully you know about me and my extended family by now, because I'm about to tell you a story that isn't exactly "NORMAL?", but I'm pretty sure that's exactly what you've been expecting.

One

Whenever one of life's unforeseen twists and turns curled its way onto the path in front of us, Mother would always say, "When you come to a curve in the road, bend with it."

Of course, it's Mother, so the quote would continue for a while. He's from New York where conversation is considered something between a monologue and a drawn-out combat sport.

"You have to be as flexible as possible when dealing with the unpredictable," he would predict. "All of life may be a circle, but there are still some difficult corners you have to get around. You need to expect the unexpected if you are going to adapt to the law of surprise and demand.

"It's always important to remember that the Circle of Life is actually just one big learning curve."

As you've probably realized by now, Mother's a bit of an idiom savant. His turn of phrase is usually a bit of homespun (with the emphasis always on the pun) wisdom that he's quite adept at.

Not that long ago, however, Mother unexpectedly found himself, or perhaps lost himself, suffering from the parental nightmare of empty nest syndrome. His home-spun wisdom spun out of control. He became disjointed, unnerved, unable to bend, unable to sway with his idiom-atic curve.

With the last of his children, my youngest siblings, the twins Chip and Dale, having moved out of his and Dad's home in rapid succession, for the first time since my mother died, there was no one left in the house to be Mothered. That left his homemade bread the only thing in the house that needed to be kneaded. And Mother needed to feel needed.

Mother never met a metamorphosis he was comfort-able with. So, unable to morph with the changes sur-rounding him, he was lost in transition. When you care for the world, it's hard to live without a care in the world. Our Mother hen couldn't help but brood about the fact that he no longer had a brood to brood over. He did his best to bend with the curve that life had thrown him, but all he could seem to do was sit on the stoop and stoop.

And so, he heartfully, soulfully, felt like a Mother, less child. He felt it to the point that Uncle Josh actually heard him singing that song in the kitchen on more than one occasion, as he cooked and baked far more food than the rest of the extended family could possibly eat.

At the same time, not long after Uncle Josh retired from

his congregation, and helped my brother Robbie and his husband Mark with the adoptions of their son Chris and daughter Madeleine, he also began to experience a growing urge to feel useful again. "A person is only as valuable as his net worth to his fellow beings," he would say. "Right now, I have an empty net, and an empty net holds little value to anyone."

That was never really true of course. The gentle fisherman's net was widely cast over the entire extended family, ready to ensnare any problem or concern that swam our way.

Everyone relied on him for one thing or another. But those things usually weren't the types of things that left one feeling fulfilled or necessary. The cup that usually runneth over was at best half filled. Uncle Josh desperately missed being a rabbi and all the volunteer work he did as such. He missed the difference that making a difference makes.

Not one to gather any moss however, Uncle Josh recommended that he and Mother climb out of their rut and start rolling their stones again. It was time to do something about the malaise they were experiencing. "It's time to roll out the mitzvahs. A sedentary stone gathers no más," he smiled in a twisted paraphrase.

Mother wasn't even sure what that meant, but he seldom questioned anything Uncle Josh said, so he just nodded his head in agreement. That's all his best friend needed. The rolling stones were going back on tour.

Uncle Josh suggested they visit the still active children's home, a few miles from where they lived, to see if they could volunteer. "If we're going to be useful, let's go somewhere where we can really be of some use."

Mother was apprehensive and, at first, reluctant to make the trip. He speculated that needy children are like homeless kittens: if you pick up one to see how it's doing, you come home with the whole litter. He wasn't sure how Dad would feel when he found the sum of the children's home in his own.

"Joshie, I'm still not sure that this is the best solution," Mother anxiously confessed to Uncle Josh as the two aging do-gooders set out on their plan to do good. "Kids can be sticky. What if I become attached to one?"

"I'll tell you what," Uncle Josh laughed. "If I see your biological clock resetting itself into some alternative time zone, I'll cut the umbilical cord and drag you back to the future, or at least the present. But in the meantime, we can both be doing something that makes us feel happy and useful. Let's dis the 'dis' in dissatisfaction and do our best to get some. Are you with me?"

"Have I ever not been?" Mother asked with a more-than-appropriate-reason-to-be-worried look on his face. Although he knew that their undertaking was simply to do a little volunteer work, he was convinced that he was already beginning to lactate.

It should come as no surprise that the pair secretly set out on their investigative mission to do good without telling anyone what they were doing, nor where they were heading. Mother was afraid that Dad would think he was acting foolish about the whole empty nest thing, so he wasn't willing to risk a foolish discussion unless there was absolutely something foolish to discuss. And Uncle Josh didn't mention anything to the others, because he knew the secrecy of their mission would drive Aunt Sue and Aunt Allie batty. And if there was one thing he truly enjoyed, it was driving the Misses Crazy.

And so, with Uncle Josh's resolve firmly in the driver's seat, and Mother's unarmed confidence riding shotgun, the dynamic duo embarked on their first action adventure in recent memory.

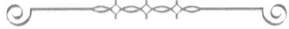

Two

When the two friends arrived at the children's home, they were surprised at just how welcoming and warm their reception was. The director of the home knew Uncle Josh from his assistance in Robbie and Mark's recent adoption of their daughter, Madeleine, and gladly welcomed any volunteering the two friends were willing to offer.

Like most institutions of its kind, the children's home was underfunded and understaffed, and, although there were only a few children left in their charge, they were still too short-staffed to meet the needs of those they had. Uncle Josh and Mother had made the director an offer he couldn't refuse, simply by making him an offer.

During their preliminary conversation, the director pointed out one boy who could particularly use some attention. His name was Surdas Patel, a blind ten-year-old originally from India who was orphaned at an early age, and came to the home after his great-aunt who brought him to this country had passed away. It was a long story that the director assured them Surdas would be more than happy to tell, as he was extremely bright and sociable, and loved to tell stories.

The director looked at his watch and said, "The boy is like clockwork. You'll find him reading one of his braille books in the garden. Reading and spending time outdoors are among the pleasures that make him tick.

"I can guarantee you that the time you spend with the boy will be time well spent," he remarked as he pointed out the direction to the garden. "Although he cannot see, he's a bit of a visionary, and he has this unique ability of being able to open up everyone else's eyes."

As it turns out, the director was not just waxing poetic in his description of Surdas. Almost from the moment of their introduction, the two volunteers understood that there was something extraordinarily captivating about this young boy. It almost seemed as though he stepped out of some exotic fairy tale, though with a saga perhaps too grim for most fairy tales not of a similar name.

Yet despite his current situation, Surdas possessed an attitude as bright and promising as any hoped-for tomorrow. Mother and Uncle Josh would later agree, that as soon as they met him, they were reminded of the enchanted boy from the "Nature Boy" song.

Surdas knew nothing of the two strangers who had interrupted his reading in the garden, yet he made them feel as welcomed as a long-awaited summer rain. When Mother asked him what he was reading, he laughed that it was a book on anti-gravity that he couldn't seem to put down. The joke was an open invitation to join him, and, within a few sentences of the unexpected introduction, the book was safely tucked away in favor of an interested audience, as Surdas enthusiastically told Mother and Uncle Josh the story of his life.

Surdas was born blind, and was named after a famous sixteenth-century Hindu poet and songwriter whom many Hindus consider a saint. That Surdas was also born blind, neglected by his family, and abandoned by age six. He managed to survive on his own throughout a spiritually based childhood, and eventually became famous for the thousands of beautiful devotional songs he composed to the Lord Krishna, many of which still survive today.

The current Surdas also suffered from neglect, though perhaps a bit more benign than his namesake. He was rescued from his village in Northern India by his elderly great-aunt, who lived in America. She learned that the three-year old's parents had died, and that he was living in squalor in a run-down orphanage in what was left of his ransacked village.

In the six years that he lived with his elderly relative, she lovingly cared for him, and taught him much. She was the first kindness that he remembered. She seemed to innately understand both the limitations, and lack of such of his blindness. She compassionately helped them both learn from, and cope with, his condition extremely well, so that he wouldn't feel different, or like he didn't fit in.

Surdas's great-aunt taught him, as best she knew how,

to assimilate as an American child before he started school. Although she was forced to send him to a special school for the blind, she mainstreamed him socially by bringing him to playgrounds, and pools, and any other place she could think of where there would be plenty of sighted children his age, so that he could learn to adapt and assimilate.

Wherever they went, his great-aunt would describe everything in such vibrant detail, that he could imagine it vividly in his mind. His perceptions were so on target, that whenever he discussed whatever was in his mind's eye with other children, they were amazed at the detail in how much he somehow saw. Her vision gave sight to his. She helped him to feel accepted, and gave consistent light to his constant darkness.

However, the shadows of her age and failing health began to grow larger and darker in their last year together.

On the darkest day of the blind boy's life, he went into his great-aunt's room to wake her, and she didn't stir. He immediately knew he was in trouble. He knew his life would once again have to change. He just wasn't sure by how much. He was so afraid of being sent back to his village in India, he didn't tell anyone of her death for two days. When his school called to find out why he missed class, the frightened boy broke down and cried the truth.

That evening he was placed into child protective custody, and eventually wound up at the children's home, where once again he felt different and like he didn't fit in. Once again, he was alone in the dark.

That was a little over a year ago. A few of his young peers had come and gone since then, hopefully to good homes where they would spend the rest of their childhood. But as interesting as he tried to make himself, nobody seemed interested in a blind Indian boy.

"Either they don't know how to deal with my blindness, or I'm not as cute as they say I am," he smiled. And then trying to lighten the mood he joked, "Perhaps that's why they haven't given me any mirrors in my room."

Mother tried to hide his sniffles and assure Surdas that he was a regular Sabu, before realizing that the boy would have no possible reference to the actor or his movies, from a time before even the boy's parents were born. And since an allusion to the *Jungle Book* character Mowgli, who was raised by wolves, might not sound as complimentary as it was intended to be, he had to awkwardly let his rush-to-his-defense go with a reassurance that they didn't lie about how cute Surdas was.

"You're like this dashing little maharaja," was the best he could come up with, hoping it wouldn't sound too politically or socially incorrect.

Uncle Josh, who was also deeply touched by Surdas's story, was curious about Surdas's life before his aunt brought him to this country, and asked him if he knew what happened to his parents.

"I am pretty much in the dark about that subject, in more ways than one," he confessed in all seriousness. "All my great-aunt would tell me was that my father died during some sort of ethnic violence that destroyed most of my village, and that my mother got gravely ill soon after from some disease that I was fortunate enough not to catch.

"I don't remember my parents being around all that much when I was little. Our village was extremely poor, and everyone, even the children, had to fend for themselves. At least that's how my great-aunt explained it.

"She told me she wanted to fill my thoughts with beauty, not tragedy, and certainly not innuendo or rumors from unreliable sources about all that happened in my village. She said, 'Every picture may tell a story, but not every story need paint a picture.' So, she would not allow me to dwell on conjectures based on baseless conjectures. She told me the most important thing to remember, was that my parents must have been very wonderful people to name me after such an important saint. She said, that as I am a product of their love and thoughts, that is where I will find their true selves in me. Therefore, all I need to know, I already know.

"She was an incredibly wise woman. As I grow older, I consistently find more meaning to the meanings she gave me. The last thing I remember her telling me is, 'It is better to be blind than to have sight, but no vision.' I try to remember when I am lonely that I still have the vision she gave me."

"I can't imagine anyone so personable being lonely," Mother remarked. "Don't you have many friends here at the home?"

"There are not many children my age here. Fortunately, most of them have found homes. The few that remain, have their sight, and find more time to tease than pay attention to someone who is sightless.

"I guess there are many ways to be an easy target. For instance, because I can't see them, they like to poke at me from all directions. And when I complain and ask them to stop, they say things like, 'Why? Can't you be touched? Are you an untouchable? Surdas can't be touched because he's an untouchable.'

"As cruel as that sounds, I truly don't believe that they understand the hurt in that term. I suppose there are many ways to be blind. And I actually don't hold their lack of any understanding against them.

"It's important not to lose sight of how important sight is when you're young. It's not like I'm going to be much help playing sports or doing much of anything else that's active. And kids my age are usually pretty active. It's the whole *the fault is not in the stars, but in ourselves* thing.

"So, I spend most of my time reading, braille of course, and listening to educational programs on the radio or TV. They help in preventing tunnel vision, and bring enlightened images to a mind that needs all the help it can get."

"You are quite an amazing young man," Uncle Josh replied, "as intelligent as anyone twice your age. I can't begin to tell you how much I have enjoyed our conversation. I hope you'll allow us to spend more time with you when we return."

"I take it you gentlemen are some sort of volunteers," Surdas smiled, a little disappointedly, "and not an older gay couple looking to foster or adopt."

"Actually, Joshie is straight and a bit older than me," Mother said, in amazement, "but I must say that otherwise you're very perceptive."

"You learn a lot by just listening when there are no other distractions," Surdas replied. "For instance, I can tell by your manners of speech that you are both from New York City. Mr. Joshie is Jewish, well-educated, and probably some sort of teacher. He speaks as one who has spoken in front of many people before.

"I'm quite sure from your answer that you're gay. You're extremely sensitive because you were sniffling when I was telling you my story, and you're not now, so you don't have a cold. And if you will forgive me for saying so, I can tell by the noise from your chair that you're a bit heavier than Mr. Joshie."

"Let's just say that black was considered thinning until I got hold of it," Mother confessed. "Now when I go shopping, the fitting room barely does."

The comment drew a huge smile from Surdas that morphed into uncontrolled laughter.

"I can also tell by your questions and responses," he added, regaining his composure, "that you've had children before, and you're probably missing them now."

"Amazing!" Mother cried. "You're like some sort of personality savant. How do you know so much about manners of speech and Jewish and gay people?"

"Like I said," Surdas smiled, "I read a lot and I listen to a lot of programs ... mostly PBS and NPR. But, to tell the truth, I also listen to TV shows like *Glee* and *Ellen* a lot too."

"Isn't Ellen wonderful?" Mother gleefully replied, at someone sharing his talk show passion.

"Now *she's* the one who's amazing!" Surdas laughed. "She's like NPR with more laughs, a song, and, I understand, a wonderful dance."

"Joshie, this boy is —"

"Is a remarkable young man!" Uncle Josh interjected, interrupting Mother's enthusiasm. "But, as we started to say, it's time to go, Benji. We have to do the thing about the cord. Remember?"

"The cord?—Oh yeah!—Right, the cord. OK! But you'll see us again tomorrow, Surdas. You can count on it," Mother promised, as he got up to leave.

"I may not see you tomorrow," Surdas joked, "but I will count on it, Mr. Benji."

As the two men left, Surdas confidently thought to himself, *How are they going to do the thing about the cord when I'm pretty sure they don't own a pair of scissors?*

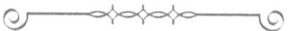

Three

Mother and Uncle Josh's heads may have been spinning when leaving Surdas, but they weren't the only ones caught up in the circle game. My husband John and I had been spinning our wheels for some time in our New York apartment, and were in desperate need of some traction. Mother's whole bend with the curves, Circle of Life, reasoning may help make him a well-rounded person, but the whole circular reasoning thing wasn't working well for either of us.

It seemed that life was throwing more curves at us than a roundabout. As I went round and round in the literary circle game, and John spun his wheels looking for a ministerial position, I couldn't help but wonder why someone doesn't invent some sort of GPS to help you navigate through life's confusing situations; something that tells you a right turn when there's nothing left, or a left turn when nothing is going right; something like a tool for someone who constantly finds himself acting like one.

Now don't get me wrong with the whole bends and curves thing. It's not that we were lost in the spin we were in, or that we had been spiraling completely out of control recently. Well maybe, because just yesterday I could have sworn that I saw a cow, a woman on a bicycle, and a girl named Dorothy whirling by our bedroom window as I twisted and turned, and tried to contemplate my next life-changing move.

Life gets complicated when life-changing decisions involve more than one life. In my family, the Poole-Hall extended family, each and every decision seems to involve more than one life. So, with everyone's lifeline so well connected, even the slightest tug or shudder on the family vine is felt by all.

Mine was not the first decision to affect the family circle in the latest round of go-rounds, nor the most major, but, in a roundabout way, its impact was almost as profound. Sales of my first book were starting to take off, and my second book was just about ready for publication. My agent was scheduling book signings, interviews, and readings. I had every reason to stay in New York City where John and I have a small apartment. I was perfectly situated for my career situation. As my agent kept on telling me, everything was happening because I happened to be where everything is happening.

The problem was that it doesn't matter how great the city you live in is, if your mind is in a bad state. Not that long ago, my mind had taken up residence in such a state, and somehow failed to leave a forwarding address. But my heart knew where it was, and everyone knows where the heart is … home.

For quite a while, John and I had been talking about accepting my brother Robbie's and his husband Mark's generous offer to build a house on their property in upstate New York. The balance of our extended family has been living in the three existing houses there for the past couple of years, and they have been urging us to join them for quite some time. And, to make things more complicated, John and I had been contemplating adding to our immediate family, so the time seemed ripe to go home.

With all that in mind, John applied for, and was accepted to be the minister in a non-denominational church a few miles from the family property. It was his first acceptance after graduation from divinity school. It was a perfect opportunity in a perfect location. He was ecstatic.

Mark, who has a master's degree in architecture, had already begun drawing up a few plans for our new home. He previously made some outstanding improvements to the three existing houses on the property, as well as substantial improvements on the homes of other clients, but this would be the first home he was going to build from scratch. He couldn't wait to sink his teeth into it. It was his dream. He was champing at the bit. He too was ecstatic.

Then there's Robbie, the other shoe that doesn't have to wait to fall. If you know me, you know that Robbie and I are extremely close. We're so close that lesser husbands would have difficulty dealing with the seamless connection between us. Fortunately for us all, that has never been a concern. The love and trust in our family is that strong and that unbreakable. The only concern was the distance that distance perpetuates. Robbie and I were especially ecstatic at the thought of putting that distance behind us.

Add all that ecstatic electricity to the normal voltage of energy that my family would be producing at the thought of us all being together again, and you can imagine my conundrum when my agent said, "Move your career to the sticks, and you might just as well use it for kindling."

It was voltage overload! My creativity blew a fuse, and the novel that I had been writing, my third and hopefully brightest, suddenly went dark. My mind became as blank as the computer screen I endlessly stared at, wondering where all the words went. The writer's block seemed more like a blockade. After a few weeks of transcendental medication, not all of it legal, I was forced to act.

Desperate tomes called for desperate measures. I knew that I was a good writer, perhaps even on the verge of becoming a great writer. In order to successfully do the write thing, I was going to have to do the right thing. I called my agent and told him that if he wanted to remain my agent, he better learn how to keep the fires burning with upstate kindling because John was going to be a chaplain, Mark was going to build a home, my family was going to be together again, and I was going to march to the beat of my own conundrum.

Life may not always reward you for making the right decision, but relatives often do. Mother, Dad, Aunts Sue and Allie, and Uncles Josh and Mohammed came up with an idea for keeping the New York apartment, by having them all share in the cost of the rent. For the older adults, it would be sort of a New York City retreat for anyone who wanted to visit the old concrete sod. And for me, it would be the write place at the right time when my career demanded that I had to be there.

John and I knew that my family would hardly ever use the apartment, and only agreed to share the cost of keeping it in order to make my life easier. But that's a perfect example of the type of love that had us moving home in the first place. That's how my family turns obstructions into constructions, stumbling blocks into building blocks, and makes aunt hills out of mountains. As Mother likes to say, "If you're looking for a way to pare rent, you'll find it in a parent."

John and I found that and more. We moved back into my parents' house while ours was being built. The family welcomed us back with open hearts and open alms for whatever the need be. We found more than the rent in parent. We found the love in family. And if you're spelling family without love firmly centered in the middle, you're spelling it incorrectly.

Four

On the way back to the car after their first visit with Surdas, Mother put his hand on Uncle Josh's shoulder and said, "Thanks, Joshie! I guess you could tell that I was getting a little carried away in there. I couldn't help it. He's such a good kid, quite remarkable. How can your heart not go out to him? You probably cut the cord just in time—"

"There's no *probably* about it Benji. I did it for us, not just you. You can't help but want to help the child. He's a ten-year-old who somehow seems centuries old, and as compelling as any narrative I've ever heard. When he told us the story of the saint he was named after, it almost sounded as if it was coming more from memory than from history. I panicked when I found myself wishing that I was young enough to take the boy in … and decided to flee when I started to think that maybe I still am.

"We're not you know … young enough … neither one of us, Mr. He's Older Than Me. You conveniently left out the older by a half hour part, I noticed. The reality of the situation is that we're getting old. And, although the best part about getting old is that you're still getting old, the best part could be better.

"Face it, Benji. We're at an age when it's hard to bear anything, much less a child. And let's not forget that the boy has special needs. He is, after all, young and blind. And we're in our sixties; soon we'll be the ones with special needs."

"Isn't love a special need, Joshie," Mother interjected, "and blind? Isn't love blind … and young? Even in your sixties, love is young. So, as long as we seek it, in some ways, so are we … at least as young as we'll ever be.

"In any case, I'm sure you're right. Tom would probably flip if I even mentioned the possibility of bringing another child home. And can you imagine what it would be like for Surdas if you brought him into your house with Sue and Allie. He'd no sooner walk through the door, and he'd be caught in the strands of their dragnet. I don't know if the boy has read enough Edgar Allan Poe, or heard enough about *The Addams Family*, to prepare him for that type of experience.

"But I have to admit, it is kind of nice talking about it, like we're some sort of old married gay couple looking to feather the nest like the boy was hoping."

"We may not be a gay couple with a nest," Uncle Josh smiled, "but we've always been a couple of birds of a feather flocking together. Family is what you make of it!"

The two friends laughed and joked and talked about

Surdas all the way home, innately understanding that it had been quite some time since they felt that alive. They began to wonder if there really wasn't some sort of magic or enchantment about this boy who had so invigorated their spirits.

When they got back to their respective houses, Mother and Uncle Josh couldn't contain the urge to talk about Surdas, even though they had both resolved not to do so.

Mother was, of course, particularly effusive in his account of the experience to Dad. And he was overjoyed when Dad was incredibly supportive of his desire to volunteer and feel useful again.

"I thought you might think I was being foolish," Mother confessed. "You know, the whole mother hen, brooding, empty nest thing."

"It sounds like it's going to be very good for you, Josh, *and* the boy," Dad assured him. "Besides, what good would it do me if I put my foot down? You know you'd only stomp on it."

"Your feet *are* kind of flat after all these years," Mother laughed.

"Are you kidding? I'm probably the only guy around with arches on top of his feet," Dad smiled. "I think it's a great idea, and I'm glad to see you happy again."

"As opposed to which other dwarf?" Mother grinned.

"I'm going to play it safe and say Doc," Dad chuckled. "Just don't overdo it and stretch yourself too thin."

"If only it was that simple, Baby," Mother replied, patting his stomach, "but thank you. What a twist it is that this oversized dwarf actually wound up with the prince."

In the other house, Uncle Josh was almost as animated in his retelling of the encounter with Surdas to Aunts Sue and Allie and Uncle Mohammed. When he finished and went to his room, Aunt Sue turned to the others and said, "I guess we all know where this is heading."

"What do you mean?" Aunt Allie asked.

"It means—I don't know nothing about birthing no blind boys, Miss Scarlet, but my inner Butterfly is telling this McQueen, I'd better get my royal rear in gear because we're going to have to wing it when the baby arrives."

"I'll explain later," Uncle Mohammed said to his more-than-confused brother who actually appeared to have question marks in his eyes.

The confusion was not so surprising when you realize that we're talking about Aunt Allie. He's still trying to fathom the millions of guys that Aunt Sue must have slept with, after hearing him say that he had sex with two Brazilian men. Not quite knowing how many millions make a Brazilian, Aunt Allie is definitely the miss in misunderstanding.

Five

As I mentioned, mine was not the first decision to affect the family circle. The family complex was already in a state of upheaval before John and I made our decision to move there. A few months before Mother and Uncle Josh's visit to the children's home, my sister Dale and her girlfriend Lauren had determined that they no longer found any part of living apart agreeable to them, and they decided it was time to fly their individual coops and build a nest together. They spread their wings for the first time in their young adult lives, and rented an apartment in one of the trendier buildings in town.

Dale's twin, my youngest brother, Chip, who was beginning studies for his master's degree in law, and working part time in a nearby law office, decided that he was of an age where he too should have his own place, and followed suit in an apartment right across the hall from the girls. Although he would have to struggle a bit to make ends meet, it afforded Chip "social" opportunities that he would not feel comfortable with in our parents' home. Being both young and extremely attractive, there were many invitations, social and otherwise, coming his way. He needed an acceptable place to accept them all. It was time for the social butterfly to leave the cocoon. He too, spread his wings for the first time.

Mother, Dad, and the rest of the family understood and supported the twins' decisions, but, though they were less than ten minutes away by car and within a good walking distance, their departure left a gaping tear in the family fabric.

Mother missed cooking for, looking after, cleaning up after, and bantering with his youngest children. Dad missed their conversations at the dinner table, and the humor and smiles as they passed by each other doing their chores and obligations throughout the day. Aunt Sue missed the good-natured joking at meals and the unfolding folding banter in the laundry room. Aunt Allie missed the teasing in the garden and the constant words of encouragement at the slightest sign of discouragement. Uncle Mohammed missed the enlightened conversations embellishing the martial arts lessons they shared. Uncle Josh missed the music of their laughter and the dance of their playfulness. He particularly missed the attention in their eyes and the understanding in their smiles at story time. Mark missed their friendship and all the generous help they gave taking care of his young daughter, Madeleine, who in turn missed the youthful joy they always brought to playtime. Robbie deeply missed the younger siblings who had been with him since he first joined the family, and the warmth that just the sight of them constantly brought to his heart and his smile.

But perhaps no one missed them more than Robbie and Mark's son, Chris, who always sought their advice, spent hours in their company every day, and had sleepovers a couple of times a month with his best buddy Chip. To Chris, Chip was not just a chip off something … he was the whole block.

The short of it was, the family was hit with a curve that they weren't expecting, and they had yet to learn to bend with it.

Chris, who was most affected by Chip's departure, had an open invitation to stay over at Chip's apartment anytime he wanted. The gesture was a sincere invitation, a genuine kindness that was meant to be so much more than the imposition it really was. Chris was now fifteen, an age that allowed him to easily understand Chip's desires for a more accessible personal life. He understood that as much as they enjoyed each other's company, Chip moved to town for privacy, not more buddy space, at least not the type they shared.

Chris knew that he would have to learn to adjust. With his education and obligations at school, helping to take care of his little sister, Madeleine, doing chores, and playing soccer with friends, it wasn't as though he didn't already have a lot on his plate. But with Robbie and Mark preoccupied with work, family, and the properties, and with the twins living in town, there was very little space for dessert on that plate. And who wouldn't miss dessert?

Chris still had his girlfriend Molly, of course. She was still the main confection of his affection. But they went to different schools and lived more than a few miles apart. With their studies and other extracurricular and family obligations, they were pretty much limited to weekend dates and short nightly texts and phone calls … in other words, dessert most weekends, desert during the week. Emotional diets are the hardest to maintain.

The whole of Chris's life was still wonderful. He still had an extended family who loved him and that he loved very much. But, the twins' leaving left a hole in the whole that was deeply felt and difficult to fill. Chris did his best to maintain his winning smile through the ordeal, but at the mere mention of the twins, it would uncontrollably slip down in the opposite direction, and his tear ducts would swell with the droplets of bittersweet memories.

If the eyes are the windows to the soul, then Chris's soul was drowning in an ocean of blues. Fortunately, his silent struggle to stay afloat did not go unnoticed. Robbie and Mark's love for their son was deep enough for them to have a heart-to-heart talk with Chris without anyone ever having to say a word. They heard the hurt he could not speak, and came up with an idea that turned out to be the perfect salve.

Robbie knew how much Chris and his schoolmates loved practicing soccer, but, due to a lack of resources, all they were able to do was practice, never actually play the game. There was neither a venue for real instruction, nor one for competition, because their high school had neither the funds nor the manpower to field a team.

As often as he could, Robbie would watch the kids practice within their small circle of friends. He knew that they were familiar with most of the rules, but their play was haphazard at best. They needed leadership from someone who truly understood the game.

Chip was a soccer star in high school. He knew the game as well as anyone, and had a personality and charisma that would lend itself well to coaching.

Robbie understood that there were many constraints on Chip's time, but he asked him if he could spare just a little of it to give the kids pointers occasionally. He told him that it would mean a lot to the boys, but it would mean the world to Chris who deeply missed his buddy and hadn't been the same since he left.

When Chip realized how much Chris missed their time together, he more than raised the ante. He played the biggest Chip he could. He volunteered to coach Chris and his friends, to help them form a team, and to find funding for it at Chris's school.

Between his studies and his part-time job, Chip was about to surrender a huge portion of the little that was left of his social life, the main reason he moved into town in the first place. But if there is anything bigger than Chip's libido, it's his heart. He loved his nephew. Chris was always his little buddy. Actually, except for Dale, he was his best buddy. Chip was about to fill into the gap. And just to make sure that there was now a whole in Chris's heart, he roped the best soccer player on his high school's girls' team into volunteering to be an assistant coach.

Chris and his new teammates were now under the soccer tutelage of Chip and Dale, or as Chip occasionally referred to them in the locker room, Chip and Dip. Fortunately for Chip, what happens in the locker room stays in the locker room.

Six

The next day after their initial visit, true to their word, Mother and Uncle Josh went back to visit Surdas. When he heard them coming toward his room, he went to the doorway and smiled. "You told me I could count on your return, and now I can finally stop counting. Though I must confess, there were too many heartbeats between the time that my friends left and came back, to keep an accurate count. Please come in. Unless I've been robbed, there are a few chairs around here somewhere."

Mother was about to answer when Uncle Josh explained that Surdas was joking. "I knew that," Mother replied. "Well, almost anyway."

"Almost is better than most," Surdas laughed. "Few people get my humor. I think that it's too NPR for them. All things considered, I'm a little too *All Things Considered* for most."

"You're trying to get us to say you're amazing again, aren't you?" Mother replied, somewhat amazed.

"No, at least not consciously," Surdas giggled. "But please feel free to express your honest opinion."

"Are you sure you're only ten?" Uncle Josh asked, with a grin Surdas could hear. "There seems to be at least a dozen or so missing years somewhere."

"I have lived many years in the ten I have," Surdas said. "But by the calendar, I believe it is still only ten."

As the threesome all took seats in the far corner of Surdas's room, he said to his seniors, "Yesterday I told you some of my story so that you would know me better. Today, I would be incredibly happy if you would tell me some of yours, so that I may know both of *you* better."

Over the next few hours, Mother and Uncle Josh told him as much of their life stories as they could squeeze into that amount of time. In what seemed to them little more than scratching the surface, they still managed to travel from the time they were born to the day they came to the children's home. Nothing or no one that they could possibly think of was left out of their accounts. By the time they were finished, Surdas was more than enthralled, and knew enough about the family history to write a book.

"Your stories are like charms from a book of enchantment," he exclaimed. "They are magic to my ears. I feel as though Scheherazade has been reading to me from *The Arabian Nights*. I would love to learn more about these famous impersonations and drag shows. And I would also enjoy more stories from your exotic travels to the far west of the country, and the Meccas for gay people at the Cape of Provincetown and the Island of Fire. Your lives and those of your family sound so exciting and magical. It's a wonder that such fortunate gentlemen have time to spend with someone like me."

"But you should realize that you're much more magical than anything we have told you," Mother said, once again rushing to the boy's defense.

"If I were magical," Surdas offered, "I confess that I would enchant you into letting me meet this exciting family of yours."

"Why do I get the feeling that you already have?" Uncle Josh replied with a smile. "I would suggest that we should perhaps wait a spell, but it may already be too late for that. I have a feeling that the spell has already been cast. We'll talk to the director, and see what we can do."

"I would be truly honored, Uncle," Surdas replied. "I have already begun to know your marvelous family through your words. I would be pleased to meet them all through theirs."

"Sometimes you speak like you're the one right out of *The Arabian Nights*," Mother observed. "How did you know that everyone refers to Joshie as Uncle?"

"In India, everyone who deserves respect is referred to as either auntie or uncle, Uncle. And as to being out of *The Arabian Nights*, perhaps you are right," Surdas smiled, as he rubbed the lamp on the table between them. "We'll see if my first wish is granted."

The following weekend, Mother and Uncle Josh received permission to take Surdas on an outing. They took him, of course, to meet the family as he requested. Surdas chalked up wish number one.

Seven

Finding funding in a town that is supporting a community college, two high schools, two middle schools, three grammar schools, and a few preschools is not easy. Chip and Robbie explored every option possible for funding a soccer team, but found minimal sponsorship in a community already stretched to the limits.

They managed to remain as charming as they were persistent, however, and were soon able to come up with many of the bare necessities as far as balls and equipment. They even managed to encourage the high school and the parents to share the costs of transportation for a team. With that accomplished, they were able to drum up some meager financial backing from a few of the establishments surrounding the school. But, by far and away, their greatest success, as far as financial support, came from the silent backers in the not-so-anonymous Poole-Hall extended family, complemented with the promise of a super cool gift of uniforms made by the Little Shoppe of Hoarders, aka Aunt Sue and Aunt Allie.

When the aunts first approached Chip with the idea of making uniforms for the team, he wasn't all that sure that the seemly seamstresses of flashy drag regalia were the best solution. There may be a boy in the middle of flamboyant, but flamboyant isn't usually the goal on a soccer field. However, since there weren't any worse solutions, never mind better ones, he had little choice. The only solution appeared to be in the aunts' resolution to help.

Reluctantly, Chip gave in to the offer, but only after asking Aunt Sue multiple times if he was sure he knew what he was doing in designing uniforms for high school boys.

"Of course, Sweetie," Aunt Sue eventually replied. "If anyone knows how to make clothes that look good, wear well, and that you can run fast in, it's a drag queen. If we can make costumes that do that in heels, imagine what we can do with uniforms in flats. We have tons of material left over from our old performing days. Allie and I are the original material girls when it comes to making costumes. The only difference between a costume and a uniform is the length of the pants and the amount of crotch outline you allow to show."

"What? Wait! No outlines, there are no crotch outlines, just shorts and shirts. Are you absolutely sure you know what you're doing?" Chip nervously pressed.

"There are absolutely no absolutes, Baby," Aunt Sue smiled. "But absolutely! We'll make you a couple dozen uniforms in sequence that will knock your soccer's off."

"Wait! What?" a confused Chip asked.

"Don't worry, Sweetie," Aunt Sue laughed. "Your auntie knows the difference between sequence and sequins. Unless you want me to design a uniform just for you, in which case, I might get confused."

"You knew you'd scare me, didn't you?" Chip apprehensively smiled back.

"Of course, Baby. You've got to hone your edge if you want to stay sharp, and if your auntie was any sharper, you'd be bleeding."

The gamble paid off. Aunt Sue's and Aunt Allie's honed-made, sharper than sharp results were super cool uniforms that any sports player in just about any sport would be proud to wear. With accentuating lightning strikes amid a hail of soccer balls on a green soccer field, and a well-placed goal, on the shirt, not on the pants, the aunts called their creation "Eclectricity."

Aunt Sue and Aunt Allie even brought one of the uniforms to the largest department store in the mall, and convinced them of the great advertising that donated complementary green socks and soccer shoes would bring to such a cool uniform, with the store's logo prominently displayed on the back of each shirt.

Chip wasn't sure if he could coach his team into winning shape the first year of play, but the aunts certainly had them looking the part. The "Eclectricity" team looked more than charged and ready for action.

Much to Chip and Dale's delight, and perhaps surprise, Chris and his teammates were better soccer players than they had ever imagined. The school board was so impressed with their workouts, that they worked out a schedule with the conference in the surrounding area for the upcoming season.

With opening day only a few weeks away, the team was almost set. The only position the team seemed weak in was goalie—unfortunately, the worst position to be weak in. None of the players they tried out at that position were even close to working out. The twins were getting worried about their team's chance for success. It was then that Uncle Mohammed came to the rescue.

After watching the team practice for weeks before the season started, Uncle Mohammed asked Chip and Dale why they weren't using their best goalie.

"We don't have a best goalie," Dale responded. "For all practical purposes, we don't even have a goalie."

"What's the matter with Chris?" Uncle Mohammed asked.

"Nothing!" Dale answered. "Chris is a striker, our best player on offense. He's by far our leading scorer."

"A team that has to rely strictly on scoring is offensive at best," Uncle Mohammed joked. "You should know from your training with him, that Chris is probably also your best player on defense. No team wins without a good defense, and even the best defense is not a good defense without a good goalie."

"What makes you so sure that Chris will be a good goalie?" Chip asked.

"Because, as you are well aware, Chris is a master at

defending himself," Uncle Mohammed responded. "The only difference between his martial arts training and the goalie position is the weapon of his opponent. In this case, the soccer ball is a larger, and therefore easier, weapon to defend against, than some of the others with which he has trained.

"Why don't you try him out? You have little to lose. If I am right, your offense may suffer a little, but you will have an excellent goalie and an excellent soccer team … something you don't have right now."

"And if you're wrong?" Dale asked.

"The good part is, as I have said, you have nothing to lose," he smiled, knowingly. "The better part is that I'm not wrong."

Chris was better than even Uncle Mohammed had expected. He had an uncanny ability to determine which way the opposing player would try to kick or head the ball, and always seemed to be in the right position to make the save.

Uncle Mohammed had taught him during their martial arts lessons, that his opponent would do everything he could to mask the secret of his next move, but the eyes always have it. He said, "The eyes will reveal what everything else will conceal. Watch for their direction and you will know yours. Don't be deceived by last second distractions meant to mislead you. The true intent will gleam in your opponent's eyes."

Even the twins, who were excellent scorers when they played, failed to get a ball past Chris once he took to the goal. They also knew Uncle Mohammed's advice, and would try to deceive Chris with their eyes, but they couldn't mislead their young goalie. He could read the intent in the slightest glance. They even tried using sunglasses to no avail. His instincts were that good. They couldn't be prouder of their nephew. The more they beamed, the better Chris seemed to get.

Chris's star was never brighter, nor was the outlook for his team. And since soccer goalies traditionally wear different shirts than the rest of the team, the aunts designed a special uniform for Chris to make him appear more fearsome.

His uniform was black, with the same accentuating lightning strikes as the other players, but with red and white soccer skulls and the goal on the shirt with a prominent "DO NOT ENTER" sign hung above it. The "O's" in "DO" and "NOT" were flaming soccer balls, and the ground on either side of the goal was littered with the ashen remains of balls that tried and failed against its keeper.

Chris's uniform was almost as awesome as he was. The whole scenario was so shocking, that they took the name The Shockers. And they weren't done shocking … not by a long shot.

Eight

In the middle of all this family upheaval, John and I moved into Mother and Dad's house. It would be months before our house was completed, but it hardly seemed fair for us to remain in the comforts of the City, while the rest of the family worked hard in preparing a home for us. Besides, John was excited about getting acquainted with the church where he was to become minister. There could be no better way to familiarize himself with his new surroundings, than to be able to spend some time with the current minister, who was about to retire.

I thought it would be strange living back in my parents' home again, even if it were just for a while. Strange, but at least this time John and I wouldn't have to sleep in separate rooms.

Mother and Dad made the move easier than expected, by giving us all the space we needed, while still providing just about every need we could possibly have.

With Mother, Dad, Chris, and the aunts and uncles just

doing the normal things they normally do, all the cooking, cleaning, laundry, shopping, and chores were pretty much taken care of. Both John and I each had but one item on our to-do lists. Everyone seemed to insist that I remain focused on my writing, and John should concentrate on his new position. It appeared we found more heaven than haven when we moved in.

It took less than three weeks for us to pack up everything we would need from our small apartment. We left behind the bare necessities for maintaining the city apartment, and were able to supplement anything we left behind with whatever was in storage from the other households. Since we were only furnishing a room at the time, it was actually quite easy.

John and I moved into Dale's old room, which was slightly larger than Chip's. The extra space worked well for us, which was good because it wasn't as if we had a choice. Chip's room was already occupied.

Nine

Nobody thought much about Mother and Uncle Josh's plan to bring Surdas home for a visit, except Aunt Sue who always seems to recognize the handwriting on the wall. Probably, because he writes most of it himself. Even Mother's idea of having a full family barbeque in March didn't strike anyone else as anything beyond normal. With everyone's attention being distracted and diverted in so many different directions, the barbeque was the most welcome distraction of all. So, there was no impetus or desire for second thoughts ... only second helpings.

Uncle Josh went to pick up Surdas while Mother prepared the feast. On the drive back to the house, Surdas asked, "Uncle Joshie, if it is not too bold, may I request a favor of you?"

"Of course you may, My Boy," Uncle Josh responded. "What can I do for you?"

"Before I ask the favor," Surdas began, "do you prefer

that I call you Rabbi Joshie, since rabbi means teacher, and you are obviously a great teacher who has earned his title?"

"I would actually prefer if you called me Uncle Josh, like the rest of the family does," he responded, "but only if you are comfortable enough to do so."

"It is an honor I have done nothing to earn, Uncle," Surdas smiled, "but I would be genuinely happy to do so."

"That will make two of us, Surdas," Uncle Josh said. "Now, what is the favor that I can do for you?"

"I am asking this of you, because I know that you are wise enough to understand.

"Most people think that if you have a handicap, you are handicapped and need everything done for you. That is not the case. They are really two different things. The majority of people with handicaps need very little help, and prefer to be treated that way. But, it is not always an easy transition for everyone else when the handicap is visible like mine. It is only natural to want to help. I understand that. In that way, I am no different than they are, but, in most other ways, I am also no different than they are, and don't need to be treated differently. So, you see the only vision I lack is with my eyes.

"I often use humor about my blindness to try to put people at ease. But it helps if I also show them that I see more than they realize, by telling them something humorous or flattering about themselves that they wouldn't expect me to know, even if it's merely guessing who they are. It helps others to understand that people with disabilities still have abilities.

"It is my fondest wish to be treated as normal as any other guest when I meet your magical family. If you will help me to meet each one individually, I will do my best to joke with each one of them, and guess who they are. Perhaps that way they will be comfortable enough with my blindness to understand that there is more to me than meets the eyes."

"Although I will certainly do as you ask," Uncle Josh assured him, "I must tell you that you will find none of that is necessary with this family. You will not be treated as normal as any other guest, but rather as uncharacteristically different as any other member of the family. The only handicap you will have, will be dealing with being the center of attention, and then, only because of your newness, not your blindness. However, I'm sure that they will enjoy the humor and guessing game, as their motto goes something like, 'All for fun, and fun for all.' Just remember to relax and be yourself. That's the person everyone is looking forward to meeting."

"Don't worry, Uncle," Surdas smiled. "It's the only one I brought with me today."

"Are you sure you're not that sixteenth-century saint, miraculously squeezed into a ten-year-old boy?" Uncle Josh smiled in amazement.

"It is one of the things I am most sure of," Surdas smiled, "especially when I sing one of his poems. It is said he had a voice that the birds would envy. Only the crows would envy mine. Of course, that doesn't stop me."

"That's my boy," Uncle Josh laughed. "Off key or on, the only key to singing is to enjoy it."

When Uncle Josh arrived with Surdas, the entire family, minus John and me, but plus Molly and Lauren, were waiting to make him feel welcome. At Uncle Josh's insistence, one by one, each person stepped up for an introduction, and Surdas attempted to guess who they were, based on the stories that Mother and Uncle Josh had told him.

The first hand he took he guessed correctly as Aunt Allie, whom he respectfully referred to as Auntie Allie.

"How did you know that?" Aunt Allie asked amazed.

"Well, your hands are large and soft, and, if you'll excuse me for saying this, you have the scent of patchouli and tabouleh about you, which means that you are either the one they refer to as Allie Kat, the Persian Kitty, or one of the pretty lesbian girls. Since you said, 'Isn't he just adorable?' in a hoarse seductive voice as you stepped forward, and you have large, manicured hands, it was a pretty safe guess that you were the famous entertainer who impersonates other famous entertainers."

Surdas drew a warm hug from Aunt Allie, and heard laughter in the background. He beamed and relaxed, knowing that his humor was working. The next hand he guessed correctly was Chris.

"I have the pleasure of meeting one of the newest members of the family, young master Chris," he began. "I can tell because your hands are strong like an athlete, but not much older than mine. There is both strength and gentleness about them, which is the sign of a great soul.

I've heard many wonderful stories about you. Your hands tell me the stories are all true. I hope I get a chance to know you better."

"It's a deal," Chris, who was visibly flattered, promised, "and we always keep our deals around here. Let's sit next to each other when it comes time to eat so we can get to know each other better."

"I look forward to it," Surdas smiled.

The next hand confused Surdas, and he confessed that he wasn't sure.

"This is my girlfriend, Molly," Chris offered.

"Of course," Surdas replied. "I should have guessed by their warmth and gentleness. And may I say that I hear you are extremely beautiful."

"Did Mother or Uncle Josh tell you that?" Molly asked blushing.

"No!" Surdas replied. "Chris's voice did."

Molly turned and gave Chris a big kiss, and Chris turned back to Surdas and said, "We are so buddies!"

Next, Surdas had no trouble guessing, "This must be Uncle Mohammed, with the strong hands of a martial arts expert," he said, as he shook his hand and joked, "Please, kind Uncle, I hope you won't flip me just because you detected my blind spot."

"I have a feeling you don't really have one," Uncle Mohammed smiled, "but we can work on it sometime just to make sure."

"It would truly be an honor. And may I say that your voice has a beautiful smile that most certainly must be matched by one on your lips. I sense a man of great understanding and faith."

Next, he guessed, "These are the well-manicured ringless hands of Mother's very handsome younger son, Mr. Chip, whom so many men find so attractive."

"Are you coming on to me, young man?" Chip teased.

"Give me a couple of years to figure things out, Mr. Chip, and we'll see," Surdas teased back, "or at least you will, anyway. But maybe I should make my reservation now. I understand the lines are quite long."

At the next hand he guessed correctly, he remarked, "This is the hand of a woman who is both beautiful and athletic. I'm presuming this is Miss Dale. But you don't smell like patchouli or tabouleh," he laughed, "so you better tell your girlfriend that you're not really a lesbian."

"I love this kid," Dale gushed, while gently punching his shoulder. "You're hysterical, Surdas. Can I keep you? I'll feed you yogurt and couscous, and dress you up like k.d. lang."

"Would I know the difference?" he shrugged with a smile. "But I take it back … Your girlfriend is safe. You're pretty much a lesbian."

"My girlfriend and I thank you," Dale laughed.

"The person behind you," he said to Dale as she started to step away, "is wearing way too much perfume and still smells like the barbeque sauce that he spilled on his clothes before I got here, so I'm guessing that your brother, Mr. Chip, is trying to play a joke by getting back in line."

"Damn, this kid is good," Chip laughed, as he patted

Surdas on the back and got off the greeting line. "I thought for sure he would have guessed Lauren."

"Hey!" she shouted from the next position in line and giving herself away.

"It's OK, Miss Lauren! Rest assured that I would not have missed another beautiful flower from the same garden as young Miss Molly," Surdas assured her.

Next, Surdas had no trouble guessing Dad correctly, nor in finding appropriate compliments about his gentle and compassionate nature.

"These are hands of glue. The hands that hold a family together. It is little wonder that the family bonds are so strong here. It is an honor to meet the other patriarch of the family."

Then, before anyone said or did anything, Surdas placed his hand on his heart, and gave a humble bow.

"Without need of a word or a touch, I can tell that I am in the presence of great love and kindness," he said, his voice choking. "It can only be Mr. Robbie and Mr. Mark approaching with their little daughter, Madeleine. It is truly an honor to meet the heart of such a wonderful family. I have heard much about you from Uncle Josh and Uncle Benji, whom you call Mother. Everything that my senses tell me, tells me that they did not exaggerate your hearts or your graciousness."

"That's more than kind of you, Surdas," Robbie said as he shook Surdas's hand, "but I know my family, and I think they may have exaggerated quite a bit."

"There is more to a person than that which meets the

eye, or resounds in the ear, kind sir. Your elders prepared a wonderful canvas, but the souls of you and Mr. Mark painted a magnificent masterpiece before you even came close. There is, to be sure, beauty that you can see; but there is also beauty that you can feel. I do not exaggerate when I say that I felt the beauty of your soul and that of Mr. Mark as soon as I arrived.

"And please forgive me, kind sirs, for not addressing you both with the respectful title of Uncle. It is only in deference to your youth that I neglected to do so. However, if you will allow me to place beauty before age, it would be my honor to remedy the situation."

"What about me?" little Madeleine asked impatiently.

"Although you are only, let's see … four," Surdas began, "I see that you are already the fairest princess in the land. People from miles around marvel at your beauty and intelligence, and know someday they will say they knew you before you became a famous star. I'm just not sure if it's a movie star or a powerful star like the president. But what am I thinking? It's probably both."

"And I wonder who you're going to guess the only one left is?" Aunt Sue said in a neglected huff.

"Does not every sky have its brightest star? Does not every treasure have its greatest jewel? Is the best not always saved for last? I would never have offended such a star, such a jewel, by addressing him any sooner, Auntie."

"OK Baby, you can stop," Aunt Sue gushed. "You had me by the jewel part. I'd say it may be a little over the top, but who am I to argue with such a perceptive child. Besides, you must know that I'm going to want you to put all that on my answering machine. It does have a certain ring to it. Just don't forget to add the part where they add their phone number at the end, in case I want to call them back."

Surdas had more than accomplished his mission by the time the introductions were over. With the aid of Uncle Josh's coaching on the trip over, he even managed to have Aunt Sue wrapped around his little finger before the family sat down to eat.

To be sure, the whole family seemed to find him fascinating. And every one of them sincerely enjoyed his company, particularly Chris, who, within the space of a few hours, was already beginning to sound like an older brother willing to have his younger sibling tag along on any of his outside activities.

Surdas knew little about soccer, but Chris enthusiastically volunteered to teach him and bring him to games. "It will be easy," Chris promised. "Once you get down the basics, you'll understand everything that's going on just by listening to someone describing the play. We can make a diorama on one of the picnic tables, and I can teach you soccer by touch. It will be like we are playing a board game that you can then imagine with bigger pieces playing on a field. Then you can come to some of my matches, and my dads, or Molly, or one of the other family members can describe what is happening. We can even go to other games together, and I'll do the play by play for you."

"I do not know if I will be allowed to do all these amazing things with you," Surdas said excitedly, "but just thinking about them makes me feel happier than I have felt in a long time."

"Remember what I said," Chris responded, assuredly. "It's a deal, and we keep our deals around here."

Robbie and Mark were thrilled to see Chris so animated. He was having such a good time with Surdas, he almost forgot that Molly, Chip, and Dale were there.

Mother and Uncle Josh were just as thrilled to see Surdas so excited. He was having such a good time, he forgot all the formalities, and started calling everyone by their normal family names.

Dad and the rest of the family were thrilled to see Mother and Uncle Josh so happy. They were having such a good time feeling useful again, they forgot all about the malaise that had been plaguing them the past few weeks. As a matter of fact, everyone was so happy, they almost forgot, as the evening wore on, that they had to return Surdas back to the children's home.

When it became apparent that it was past time for Surdas to leave, you could feel the shroud of regret spread over the entire family, especially their young guest.

"This is just ridiculous," Aunt Sue shouted, as the remains of the melon dessert left on the table began to fade to melancholy. "What's your last name, Baby Boy?" he asked Surdas, as he got up from the table.

"Patel, Auntie," Surdas answered, politely.

"So that's like Smith in India," Aunt Sue said, knowingly.

"You are obviously as knowledgeable as you are talented," Surdas complimented him.

"You don't have to go there, Baby," Aunt Sue said. "You've already charmed the pants off me."

"I hope for the sake of all our other guests, Auntie," Surdas smiled, "we are speaking metaphorically."

"And let me tell you something, Sweetie," Aunt Sue chuckled. "You should be glad we are, because you'd sure as hell be missing something special if we weren't.

"I have to tell you, Surdas Patel, you remind me so much of me when I was younger. You have that same savoir-flair, that l'enchantement. You know what I mean? … Bad to the bonne. But I digress! Now everyone wait here while I regress."

The Mad Hatter hurriedly left the barbeque and ran into Mother's kitchen, leaving the rest of the table in wonderland. In a matter of minutes, he quickly returned as animated as the March Hare, insisting that Mother, Dad, Uncle Josh, Robbie, and Mark come back to the kitchen with him.

When they all returned to the kitchen, written on one of the walls in lipstick was the name Surdas Patel, and the address of Mother and Dad's house with a big question mark after it, followed by a huge "HELLO" and more exclamation points than could possibly be necessary.

"What the hell is that?" a shocked Mother demanded, looking at the graffiti.

"Wall … handwriting … Hello! to the HELLO!!!! Tell me you don't recognize it," Aunt Sue insisted. "And for everyone's sake, you all better figure out what to do about it as quickly as possible. More than just that boy's heart is going to be broken when he has to return to that home. We're all smart enough to know what's going down.

"If there is one type of drag we don't do around here, it's on people's hearts. So, wake up and figure it out, people. Don't try to tell me that you haven't heard the hope in every sentence that little boy uttered since he arrived, nor the hope that our soft-headed, soft-hearted seniors here had in bringing the boy home in the first place. The puzzle has only one missing piece, Darlings. The question is 'Are you going to solve it?'"

The deer all seemed caught in the headlights as they stared at each other trying to avert the light that Aunt Sue was glaring at them.

"Poppy-time is over, my little Dorothys," he continued. "The snowflakes have fallen. It's time to wake up and pick a side of the rainbow. Either bring that child to Emerald City, or farm him back to Kansas and leave him there. You can't leave him somewhere in between. That type of twister ride is way too much for any child to handle. You've got the brains; you've got the heart … now have the courage to click your heels and do what's right."

Uncle Josh looked as though he was about to say something, but before he or anyone else could respond, Aunt Sue pressed on. "I'm probably the most hard-hearted person around here, and I'm willing to do all I can for that boy, so I can't imagine that all you softies will let him down. You guys all have hearts as light as a feather. So how in the name of all that balances are you going to send his heart back so heavy? It's Glinda time, my dears, time to rise above the crowd … let's not burst any bubbles."

Mother looked at Dad and said, "Tommy, I was thinking that if Joshie and I did most of the work, maybe —"

"Absolutely not," Dad interrupted. "In spite of what you think, most of the work is too much work for the two of you to handle. Volunteering is one thing. Raising a child at our age is quite another."

Mother and Uncle Josh looked crushed, and the rest of the family a bit stunned.

"Besides," Dad smiled, "what am I, chopped liver? I have a heart too. I'd like to be part of the process, and I'm sure Sue, Allie, and Mohammed would also like to be part of it. If Robbie and Mark don't mind yet another addition to the village they have generously allowed to settle on their property, I say we do what we can to foster the boy."

"Robbie?" Mother asked, hopefully.

Robbie wears "Yes" on his sleeve. It's almost as big as the one on his heart. Everyone knew his answer before he was asked. But he's a good husband and tries not to make too many decisions without asking Mark first. It works well because Mark never says "No" to him anyway. Robbie turned toward Mark who was sketching something on a pad. "What do you say, Mark? Are we in?"

Mark continued whatever he was doing and didn't answer. Everyone sort of looked around the room uncomfortably for what must have seemed like minutes trying to figure out what that meant and what to do next.

"Mark? Babe?" Robbie pressed. "What do you think?"

Mark held up his pad. "I think if we make these changes to Chip's old bathroom, on the staircase coming down to the main level, and on the front and back porches, Surdas will do just fine.

"Mother and Dad have a great history fostering and adopting, so they should have no problems fostering the kid, especially with us and the rest of the family as backup. So, what's there to think about?"

The room lit up in gleaming teeth as Mark continued, "Robbie and I kind of have a handful of handfuls at the moment with work and two kids, but you know we'll help as much as we can. Just keep in mind that Surdas is a ten-year-old blind boy who will need extra help with his studies and with navigating around the property early on. Everyone will need to have better than double vision to make up for the vision he doesn't have. But I say that as a challenge, not as a warning or deterrent. If everyone chips in, none of us, including Surdas, should have any problems."

Mother gushed, "I'm so happy I don't know who to kiss first."

"Hey, I think I'd make a good start," Mark volunteered, still holding up his sketches. "Though I would imagine Dad and your son probably have first dibs," he smiled, somewhat embarrassed by his enthusiasm.

"A sketch in time, gets nine," Mother joked, as he hugged and kissed him. "Besides, you're my son too, Baby. So, the first nine dibs are all yours."

After a few tears and kisses, Mother looked over at Aunt Sue, hugged him, kissed him, and said, "I can't even begin to thank you for pulling all this together. You're a godsend, except of course when you're not. But I have to tell you, I am going to buy the biggest most beautiful bouquet of flowers you've ever seen, and put them on your grave, after I kill you for writing all over my kitchen wall with your lipstick."

"Oh! Please," Aunt Sue laughed. "You don't think I'd use my good lipstick, do you? I used Allie's. That cheap crap will come off with a paper towel and water. It's easier to wax on and wipe off than anything in *The Karate Kid*."

"Do you think we should tell Surdas about our plans, or wait until we see how the process is going?" Mother asked in general.

"Neither!" Aunt Sue replied, still taking the lead. "Ask, don't tell. I think that you and Josh should take the boy aside, and ask him how he feels about the idea. He's already had a ton of people making decisions about his future. I'm sure that it would mean the world to him if just once, somebody would ask him. If he's happy with the idea, and it's pretty obvious that he will be, he can do his magic from the inside, while you do what you have to do on the outside."

After the meeting broke up, everyone on the inside tried to act like nothing was up, so everyone on the outside knew that something was. On the ride back to the children's home that evening, Mother and Uncle Josh took Aunt Sue's advice. Mother broached the subject since, if it all worked out, he and Dad would be listed as the foster parents.

"Surdas, I know this is rather sudden, but how would you feel if my husband Tom and I wanted to foster you? Actually, it wouldn't just be us. You would become part of the whole extended family, with Uncle Josh, Uncle Mohammed, Aunt Sue, Aunt Allie, Tom and I sharing in most of the responsibility of trying to raise and homeschool a ten-year-old that is smarter than us all."

Surdas gave them both a hug and said, "I would feel as if I had truly found a magic lamp and my second wish had been granted even before I wished it."

"Are you sure, My Boy?" Uncle Josh asked. "None of us are as young as we used to be. And even though Robbie, Mark, and Chris will be helping from time to time, basically you'll be surrounded by a bunch of old fogies."

"You forget that I was raised by my great-aunt, who I'm sure was older than anyone in your family, Uncle. Besides, most people consider me to be a fogey too. I'll just be a younger one. And come to think of it, none of you look like fogies to me anyway.

"You must realize what you are offering me is something that I've been wishing for, a new family. It is a blessing that is the answer to a prayer. I could not wish or pray for better. If I had my way, we'd turn the car around now and head toward my new home."

"Wonderful!" Mother exclaimed. "We're all very excited about the prospect of you joining our family. We'll start working on it right away. I know everyone in the family will try to make you very happy with your decision."

"I already am," he smiled, bouncing up and down,

unable to contain his enthusiasm. "I'm happier than you can imagine.

"And by the way, thank you for asking me how I felt about it. Nobody ever asks me how I feel about anything. They just assume that I need all the help I can get and decide for me."

"I have to confess," Mother confessed, "that it was actually Sue who told us to ask you. Can you imagine? He can be such a warm fuzzy bi-polar bear at times. I'd say he's quite an enigma, but the last time I said that, he thought it was a racial slur and wouldn't talk to me for weeks.

"Still, there's a soft heart floating somewhere between that hard ass and head. I just wish he'd think with it more often."

"Perhaps Sue's brash exterior is just another layer of makeup to hide an insecure, but caring soul." Uncle Josh offered.

"It's a beautiful sentiment, Joshie," Mother countered, "but I think that Sue's attitude is more whether related."

"Weather related?"

"Yes! Whether he wants to kill you quickly with his razor tongue, or whether he kills you slowly with kindness."

"Don't we all do what we have to do to get the attention we need?" Surdas chimed in. "Surely Auntie's actions speak louder than his words. Unlike words, actions neither lie nor conceal. My great-auntie used to say, 'Words are fiction until they are put into action. The act is the difference between a promise made and a promise kept.' I'm not sure that she meant it quite the way I'm using it, but I think it applies."

"I have a feeling Surdas isn't going to be the one getting the homeschooling," Mother laughed. "By the way, Baby, was coming here today really your first wish?"

"Yes, Uncle," he said. "It was this visit. At the time I thought that was the most I could wish for and receive. Though, I must confess, the second wish was always there, hiding somewhere behind the fear that it was too much to wish for."

Ten

Surdas moved into Chip's old room the week before John and I moved into Dale's. By the time we got there, he knew as much about the property as we did, and probably navigated it better. He was truly amazing.

Mother said that Surdas "settled in quicker than sand in a Speedo." Some of Mother's sayings you never question. It took him no time at all to familiarize himself with the layout of his room and the rest of the house. He even brought two posters written in braille with English subtitles that Mother hung up in his room on his first day. The first one read, "Don't follow in my footsteps. I run into walls," and the second, "If you don't see what you want, welcome to the club." Apparently, it was going to take Surdas a while to let go of the need for self-effacing humor.

Aunt Allie helped speed up the process a bit, however, by having the posters beautifully framed in glass as a Welcome Home surprise for Surdas. It never dawned on Aunt Allie that the boy could no longer read the posters.

Of course, Surdas didn't mind. Actions speak louder than words, even in braille, and he truly appreciated the gesture.

The rest of his hitch went without a hitch. Chris and Surdas seemed to become instant buddies. Chris treated him like the younger brother he always wanted, and loved "showing" him around the property and town. He took Surdas with him on whatever errands he ran, and he enjoyed having Surdas tag along when he spent time with his friends.

Chris really delighted in explaining as much as he could, in as much detail as possible, so that Surdas felt comfortable in his surroundings. Chris was never so full of life. It was truly infectious. The two boys loved teasing and bantering with each other. Surdas particularly took pleasure in teasing Chris about being blond, though no one remembers ever telling him that was the case.

In any case, within a few days these two very different boys seemed as close as any two brothers could possibly be.

Perhaps the most wondrous thing of all about their relationship, however, was not the effect on Chris, but the effect on Surdas. Under Chris's tutelage, Surdas became a boy again. The transformation was amazing. He stopped trying to be impressive, and became even more impressive. He became a child, allowing himself to experience the sheer joy of just being a child. What could be more heartwarming, more impressive than that?

Mother went out of his way to make sure that Chris understood how proud everyone was of the way he adopted Surdas into his circle. Chris shrugged off the accolade, and responded that it was nothing because he truly enjoyed Surdas's company. He truly believed that he was the fortunate one in their friendship.

"Much like your dads, you're a heart of gold at the end of the rainbow," Mother told Chris. "It may seem like nothing to you, but even the tiniest kindness explodes like an atom balm, to someone who needs it."

Chris smiled like he understood the comment, and just walked away a bit bewildered, knowing it was most likely another one of Mother's compliments.

Little Madeleine also took to Surdas right away, and quickly began to think of him as a second brother. She loved playing with him, and even learned how to call him on the phone to ask him to come over during story time, which he always seemed happy to do. She loved taking him by the hand, and guiding him carefully around her home, past errant dolls, storybooks, toys, and other girlie pitfalls, to secret places where candy and cookies were hidden.

Surdas pretended that they were being mischievous when they raided the loot, but always left a detailed account of their secret bounty for her parents before he left.

Mark and Robbie were more than thrilled to have Surdas come over and pretend to read to Madeleine right before her nap time. Seldom was his story finished before the nap began, but usually it was Surdas who succumbed first. Madeleine would usually finish the made-up story with a made-up ending that pleased her, and then cuddle off to sleep with her real-life teddy.

And Hopi, Robbie and Mark's blind dog, somehow

saw in Surdas a kindred spirit. She loved to follow him around, and in her own way searched for him whenever he was gone. If Surdas was anywhere on the property, Hopi somehow knew where to find him. It took less than a week for her to move out of Robbie and Mark's house and into Mother and Dad's, and begin sleeping in Surdas's bed. When Surdas wasn't off somewhere with Chris, he and Hopi were inseparable. Surdas even joked that they took turns discovering stuff around the house the hard way. "We are the things that go bump in the night," he laughed.

Eleven

Surdas was living in Chip's old room less than two days before he was spirited off by Mother and the aunts for the required shopping spree and makeover. It's sort of a rite of passage in the Poole-Hall extended family, which is a lot more nerve-racking, or perhaps nerve-wrecking, than it sounds. Clothes shopping, shoe shopping, haircut, manicure, pedicure ... it takes a sturdy character to survive the drag queen gauntlet.

"You can't play with fashion when you're sporting designer genes," Aunt Sue would laugh, as he held up numerous clothing combinations in front of Surdas. "Maybe clothes don't really make the man," he'd chuckle, "but they certainly help him get made."

It isn't easy enduring an ordeal when you can't tell whether it is costume or customary ... but Surdas survived, even the brief experience in the underwear department. The problem was, since he was blind, he just wasn't sure how well he survived.

Chris knew the drill, having barely survived it himself when he first arrived, so he was more than prepared to address Surdas's concerns when he came home, though perhaps not as seriously as Surdas would have preferred.

"Please tell me I don't look like some Bollywood drag queen," an only half-joking Surdas asked Chris as he walked through the door. "I spent the last several hours in the custody of Auntie Sue and Auntie Allie, and I don't have any idea what was done to me."

"Calm down," Chris answered, sounding serious. "You don't look like a Bollywood drag queen. But what's with the Girl Scout outfit and the red toenails and fingernails. It's a little girly, don't you think?"

"What? Are you serious?" Surdas panicked. "You're joking! Please tell me you're joking."

"OK! OK! It's not that girly. It's just not my cup of tea. But you do look cuter than you did as a boy. Do you have any cookies to go with that outfit?"

"You're having fun with me, aren't you?"

"Isn't that what friends do?" Chris laughed.

"Imagine yourself blindfolded and under the control of the aunties for hours in a spa, where several people are clipping and primping you, while calling you pet names like Rajah Ramjet, Kali Flower, Om Boy, Dahl Face, Swami River, and worst of all, Gunga Din Din, and the Little Brahman About Town. All this, after being dragged from store to store, with the aunts singing "It's A Mall World After All," and shopping and trying on clothes, many of which were too tight for even a skinny kid like me, then tell me what state of humor you would be in."

"You're right!" Chris agreed. "I'm sorry! I know what it's like when you can see what they're doing to you. I can't even imagine what it was like for you when you couldn't. I really am sorry. I wasn't thinking. I just wanted to show you that I can be funny too. But what happened to Mother?"

"I think he had to run some errands, so he told the aunties to take good care of me. So now seriously … did they?"

"You look cool, very cool. Your clothes, your haircut and even your nails, which are not red, are all very cool. I especially love your new sunglasses, which *are* red. They're super cool!"

"Uncle Benji bought them for me, because he said that I should always view the world through rose-colored glasses, even if I couldn't actually see it that way."

"You look great! I promise," Chris said seriously. "I'm even a little jealous."

"Promise me that we'll always be honest with each other, Chris, especially when it comes to the way we look."

"Does that mean no more dumb blond comments?" Chris smiled.

"I said promise me we'll be honest with each other," Surdas laughed.

Twelve

The afternoon when John and I arrived, the entire family, including Surdas and Hopi, were waiting outside the house to welcome us. After all the hugs and kisses, Surdas stepped up with his hand outstretched to greet us. When John's hand met his, something amazing happened. He slowly pulled John into a warm hug, which he held for a while, and then beamed this astonishing smile.

He kept the same smile as he took my hand and pulled me into a similar hug. He again held it for a while before he slowly pulled away, and placed his hand first on my face and then on my heart, as though to make sure of something. Then he hugged me again, as if we had known each other his entire life. He held the second hug for another minute or two, and whispered, almost inaudibly, "Bapu, I am so glad you are finally here."

"What was that, Buddy?" I asked, as the embrace unlocked.

"I apologize," he said, as though somewhat embarrassed. "I was lost in thought. I'm just very happy to meet you, after hearing so much about you. I'm glad that the wait is over, and I finally got to meet you both."

"No need to apologize," I said, finding myself almost as elated as he seemed. "John and I have heard so much about you from everyone. We're thrilled to meet you too."

And the strange part about that conversation was that we truly were both thrilled more than we imagined possible. It was more like some wonderful reunion than a first meeting. In the excitement and confusion of the moment, I forgot to ask Surdas about the strange word he whispered in my ear.

Surdas insisted on helping us unpack the van, and jokingly offered to show us the best way to navigate the layout of Mother and Dad's house without bumping into anything. John and I were amazed at just how personable and comfortable he was in his new surroundings. He had been in the house exactly a week, and yet somehow, he seemed like our host.

As a matter of fact, the only difficulty Surdas seemed to be experiencing in his new surroundings, was in the respectful manner he wished to address everyone. Mother and Uncle Josh had broken him of the habit of using the Mr. prefix before his elders' names, and he did not want to appear either presumptuous or insulting by calling John and me "Uncle." To add to his confusion, he still had no idea how to handle addressing Mother and Dad either, as their family titles carried too much respect for him to presume using them, no matter how much they insisted upon it.

Surdas knew that Mother and Dad preferred not being addressed as Uncle Ben and Uncle Tom, and Uncle Mother and Uncle Dad made even less sense to him. So, when we arrived, he was still addressing Mother as Uncle Benji, the name he had obviously picked up from Uncle Josh, and he was referring to Dad simply as Uncle.

Titles aside, it takes no time at all to settle in, when you're already home. So, after all the "Welcome Homes," the hugs, the kisses, and the unpacking, Mother prepared a wonderful buffet dinner for the entire extended family. There were three tables crowded with hot and cold dishes of remarkable variety that more than adequately addressed any dietary concerns, and every dietary desire.

Chris helped Surdas navigate each delicacy with amazing descriptions that made each one almost impossible to resist. At the end of the last table, there was a plate of matzos. Surdas smiled as he picked up one of the sheets, ran his hand across the top of the matzo, and turned toward Uncle Josh with an impish grin on his face and asked, "Uncle Joshie, who writes this nonsense? I think it says, 'Let them eat cake.'" The place cracked up, and the mood was set for the entire evening.

As the family sat down to eat, plates full, eyes wide in anticipation, Mother asked if anyone would like to offer a few words of thanksgiving. Before anyone else could respond, without any prompting, Surdas started singing a beautiful Hindi prayer that brought tears to every eye in the house, though only he understood the words that he chanted.

He had told Uncle Josh that he sang with the voice of a crow, but all anyone heard was the graceful singing of a songbird. Well beyond the length of the song, every bird-of-a-feather felt like they were a bird of paradise.

Hours into the festivities, after everyone helped clean up, including Hopi on floor detail, the family retired to the living room where Uncle Josh suggested that a story might be in order, only this time, not by him. He wanted to hear one of Surdas's favorite stories from *One Thousand and One Nights*.

"Actually, my two favorites are *Aladdin and His Wonderful Lamp* and *Ali Baba and the Forty Thieves*, both of which are in fact from the later French translation, *Les mille et une nuits*, by Antoine Galland," Surdas said as he carefully lifted Madeleine onto his lap. "Which would you prefer to hear?"

The night was as young as the captivating speaker, so Uncle Josh's answer was, "Whichever one you wish to start with first!"

"Once upon a time there was a beautiful princess named Madeleine," he said as he ad-libbed the beginning of the first spellbinding journey.

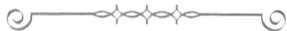

Thirteen

The next morning, Chris decided to take Surdas to his favorite place in the world, the place where he and Molly had their first picnic, and more importantly, their first kiss. It is a lake on a neighbor's property that is almost completely surrounded and hidden by pine trees, save for a huge rock formation at one end from which a waterfall, three-quarters of the way up, pours majestically down into the lake. Right above the crest there is a small overhang on which you can sit and dangle your feet into the rushing falls.

At the base of the formation, Chris instructed Surdas to take off his sandals and climb with him to the overhang.

"Are you joking, or just murderous?" Surdas asked, somewhat shaken by the thought. "Do you really think that someone who is blind and can't swim should be climbing on something he can't see, barefoot no less, to experience something else he can't see, with the overwhelming possibility of falling into something he can't save himself from?"

"Stop worrying," Chris laughed. "The answer is 'No!' to at least one of those questions, and 'Yes!' to a couple of others, but there were so many, I forget which ones. Just trust me! It's really a pretty easy climb, and I'll be behind you all the way, guiding your every step."

"Oh Lord! Why does everything you are saying sound like a recipe for disaster, with me as the main course?" Surdas moaned.

"You only think that way because you carry the ingredients around with you all the time," Chris responded. "Now come on! Live a little!"

"Why do I think that last part is prophetic?" Surdas worried, as he let Chris guide him to the base of the climb. "This is either a game of blind man's bluff, or a dangerous case of the blond leading the blind."

"Tease me all you want," Chris smiled, "but we're here to have fun. That's what I'm going to do. Are you coming?"

"Do I have a choice?"

"Always! But life is always about choosing the better choices."

"You're channeling Uncle Benji, aren't you?"

"Sometimes it's the only channel around here that gets reception. Now come on! I'll be behind you all the way, guiding your every step."

"By behind me, do you mean right behind me, or a few feet away behind me?"

"Is there any answer you don't have a question for?"

"Is there any answer you have that isn't questionable?"

"Good question! I don't have an answer," Chris laughed, ending the discussion.

The boys removed their sandals and carefully began climbing the rocks, with Chris, firmly pressed against Surdas's back, guiding each grip and step with his hands. The climb was going smoothly, and Surdas was actually beginning to enjoy the experience. There was a comfort and security that he felt being surrounded by Chris's athletic body, and having his strong hands guide each movement. He even managed to smile and crack a few jokes along the way.

Halfway up the climb, however, Surdas's bare foot stepped on something sharp, and he painfully jerked away. The sudden movement made both boys lose their grips and footing, plunging them both down a six-foot drop into the water. Surdas panicked as he sank below the surface, but Chris, who is an excellent swimmer, quickly had Surdas's head above the water, and was calmly towing him toward the shore.

"Are we already dead, or should I be thinking about killing you for trying to drown me?" Surdas nervously screamed.

"Nice way to talk to someone who is saving your life," Chris chuckled, as he helped his friend back on terra firma.

After a few deep breaths back on shore, Chris suggested, "Maybe that was a mistake. Maybe we should just take the easy way and walk around the back to the path where there is no climbing."

"Are you kidding me?" Surdas yelled. "There's a path? We took the hard way?"

"We took the fun way," Chris responded. "Where's your sense of adventure?"

"I believe it's at the bottom of the lake where you tried to put me," Surdas answered. "If you jump back in, and swim to the bottom, I'm sure you'll find it."

"Keep whining," Chris laughed, as he led the reluctant Surdas up the hill behind the waterfall. "You're practically a vineyard."

A short walk later, as they turned on a narrow path, Surdas could hear the waterfall getting louder. He wondered if dangling their feet over the side of the overhang would have as much meaning, considering that they were still soaking wet, after plunging into the lake. But he tried not to be a vineyard, and press the whine any further, as he dutifully followed his friend on the path.

"Here we are!" Chris finally exclaimed, as they turned a corner, and the spray from the falls below leapt up to greet them. "This is a small overhang right above the falls. This is the best seat in the house. You can sit here and see, and hear, and feel everything. Have a seat and enjoy the beauty of Nature at her best."

Chris held Surdas's hand, and helped maneuver him into the best position on the overhang. The two boys sat there for a while, not saying much, just taking in the sounds and the smells that surrounded them. Chris spent a good deal of the time with his eyes closed trying to experience the experience, the same way Surdas experienced it.

"Tell me what it looks like from up here," Surdas eventually requested. "Is it wonderful? Are we high up? What's below us? What is the view like?"

"We're only about twelve feet or so above the lake," Chris began. "It's actually not that high. The lake below is kind of kidney shaped, and a greenish blue color, very different from the sky, which is a cool blue with a few puffy white clouds that look like giant cotton balls. There is a small patch of green grass over to our right, where Molly and I sometimes picnic, and a thin line of reddish-brown dirt around the rest of the lake, which is surrounded by tall pine trees. Below us, the waterfall's crest pours into the deep part of the lake, and it looks like splashes of white foamy water jumping back up at you. It's very beautiful."

"It sounds like heaven," Surdas said, "only wetter. I only wish I had a better idea of what the colors and the shapes meant."

"I'm sorry!" Chris apologized. "That was pretty dumb of me. I wasn't thinking when —"

"No, no, no!" Surdas interrupted. "I'm not sure of the shapes, and I've never seen colors, but you described them beautifully. I could feel them in your voice. My great-aunt used to describe to me what different colors felt like ... cool blue, hot red, warm orange, happy yellow. She gave them mood tones, but not much more than that. You gave them life. I may not know what the colors look like, but I can understand how everything you described makes you feel. That's an exciting difference."

"Thanks!" Chris said, somewhat relieved, as he put

Surdas's hand to his face and smiled a huge smile. "Do you feel this smile? This is how you make me feel."

Surdas beamed. And although he knew it was unnecessary, he returned the smile with the same gesture, to indicate they were on the same page. "What about the birds?" he finally questioned. "You forgot to mention them, but I can hear them all around. Tell me about the birds."

"I can't see them any better than you do, Buddy," Chris responded. "They're all hidden in the trees."

"Still, they are beautiful, are they not?"

"Still, they are beautiful," Chris agreed.

The two boys sat there quietly for some time, as they continued to take in the breeze, the mist, the smells, and the sounds. Though not a word was said, they could both feel the ties that bind, weaving their souls together.

Surdas was particularly impressed by the beauty of Chris's soul. He seemed so caring, so genteel for a boy his age. Yet, he was a star athlete, a martial arts expert, and had a masculine confidence of someone far older than his fifteen years. The mixture was both exciting and comforting at the same time.

"Surdas, your feet aren't even touching the water from the falls," Chris observed, after a while. "That's part of the fun. Let me move you up a bit," he said as he got up to help.

"No! Don't!" a startled Surdas yelled as he panicked from the sudden motion. The fright caused the boy to flail his arms and inadvertently push Chris away, knocking him off balance.

Chris struggled to regain his footing and, realizing he

was losing the battle, grabbed onto the only thing available to him, Surdas's shirt, to try to balance himself. Surdas, not realizing what was happening, had no chance to steady himself. There was no time for thinking, or footing, or balance, or anything else; and the two boys again plunged into the lake ... only this time from the higher distance, and directly under the falls.

It took Chris only a few seconds longer than before to again rescue Surdas from the deeper plunge. But judging by the scare on the younger boy's face as they treaded the choppy water without speaking, it might as well have been hours.

"Are you all right?" Chris finally asked, quite out of breath and almost as frightened as Surdas, as they once again reached the shore.

"If I say yes, are you going to throw me off an even higher cliff?" Surdas asked, also breathless, but with a surprising smile.

"No! I mean ... what? You're not upset with me?" a shocked Chris responded.

"How could I be? I could feel how frightened you were, when we were in the water, and yet all you thought about was me. You kept whispering over and over again, 'I've got you Buddy! Don't worry! We're going to be fine. Don't worry! I've got you!'

"You're a hero, even if you did try to kill me twice," Surdas laughed.

"You know, both times were actually your fault," Chris interjected.

"I think if we asked the other members of the family, who was actually to blame, they wouldn't choose the poor blind boy, who didn't want to go climbing in the first place, and who never should have been exposed to that type of danger," Surdas responded confidently.

"So then, it's our secret?" Chris asked.

"Of course," Surdas smiled. "I have to protect my interests. Who else is dumb enough to teach me about adventure?"

"So now I'm dumb?"

"I don't think it's just now," Surdas quipped. "You *are* blond. Remember?"

"Wait a minute. You don't even know what blonds look like," Chris responded, while playfully poking the younger boy in the ribs.

"No! But I'm blind, not deaf," Surdas giggled, more from the poking than the joking. "You don't have to see what a blond looks like when you can hear it."

"So, you think all blonds sound dumb?" Chris posed, still poking.

"Except the ones with artificial intelligence," Surdas responded, trying to appear serious.

"Artificial intelligence?"

"You know … hair dye … the blonds who try to speak brunette."

"And all this blond stuff is all based on …?"

"It's the simple Law of Karma," Surdas laughed. "If you do or say something really dumb in a past life, you come back as a blond. Then, because you're a blond, you are bound to repeat the cycle repeatedly. It's kind of like the wheel of misfortune. I'm pretty sure that the Lords of Karma invented reincarnation, just so they wouldn't have to constantly listen to all the blond spirits complaining that they couldn't wear their sunglasses and backward baseball caps anymore."

"That's so dumb that you'll probably come back platinum."

"Wait! You mean I'm not already blond? And I have these sunglasses and everything."

"Funny, my dark-haired friend! You don't really believe any of that blond stuff, do you?"

"I'll prove it to you. Do you know the difference between someone who is blond and someone who is blind?" Surdas upped the question.

"What?" Chris asked.

"Someone who is blind knows the difference," Surdas giggled.

"You're a pretty bold kid considering we're so close to the water," Chris laughed.

"I know," Surdas said, as he quickly grabbed hold of Chris and pushed him back into the lake. The shock of the dunk swiftly turned to laughter when Chris surfaced, to find his young friend standing on the shore, shrugging and tugging on a strand of dark hair, enjoying the last laugh.

"I guess you're right," he giggled. "I must not be blond!"

Fourteeen

Later that afternoon, as the barely dry Chris and Surdas were returning from their lake adventure, Aunt Allie pulled up in his car, and beckoned the pair to get in, to begin yet another one.

"Remember that little adventure we took on the dirt road to the place where we found Mohammed?" he said to Chris. "Well, this time it's Surdas's turn."

"But —?" Chris tried to question.

"I know what you're thinking, Sweetie, but no 'buts,'" Aunt Allie cautioned.

"But it's dangerous. He's only ten and he's blind. That's not the best combination for driving," Chris argued.

"Don't be silly, Cowboy. Your butt will be the one in the saddle," Aunt Allie laughed. "Surdas's adventure comes later. There may be nothing common about my sense, but I'm a few notches above nonsense. Now, no more buts, or I'll change my mind and you'll be shotgun instead of top gun."

Chris had another but, but he sat on it. He knew that Aunt Allie was taking them to see Uncle Mohammed and the Sufis, but he couldn't figure out what Aunt Allie thought Surdas would get out of it, since he couldn't possibly see anything from the balcony viewpoint of their previous adventure.

He couldn't help but think that the beauty of it all would be impossible to describe, even if you didn't have to keep silent, which, of course, you did. Still, it was Aunt Allie's adventure to steer, though Chris would soon be the one in the driver's seat. That alone made his silence golden.

When they pulled off the main road, and Aunt Allie handed the wheel over to Chris, the unsuspecting Surdas was shocked.

"Are you sure you want to do this, Auntie?" he said, in a wide-eyed voice. "If we go anywhere near water, we'll all soon be in it just so he can save us. He's got this strange combination of water fixation and hero complex going. He treats everything like it's water under the bridge, because sooner or later, you'll be there too."

"I'm not sure what you're talking about, Sweetie," Aunt Allie said, "but I'm pretty sure it's dry all the way."

"It's just some silly kid thing," Chris assured Aunt Allie, before Surdas could respond. "Quiet back there," he said to Surdas in the backseat, "or you'll make me lose my focus."

"Oh Lord!" Surdas responded. "How many times can one person be saved in a single day? He has as much focus as a fun house mirror."

"How do you know what a fun house mirror looks like?" Chris laughed.

"I listen to enough programs to know that it makes people look the way we're going to look if you don't stay focused and keep your eyes on the road."

"You worry too much," Chris smiled.

"This from a guy who must think I'm his sorrows," said Surdas, "because he's tried to drown me twice today alone."

They drove for nearly half an hour, with Chris at the wheel and Surdas asking questions like, "Was that a bump, or some poor large woodland creature?" and "Did I just hear a little scream?" To which Aunt Allie answered, "Yes, Sweetie, but it was you."

When Chris came to a main road, and surrendered the wheel back to Aunt Allie, he climbed into the backseat with Surdas and asked, "Do I really scare you that much?"

"I want to say, yes. But I guess the answer is no. Not really," Surdas responded. "The truth is that I never had a friend I could tease and play around with like this before. Teasing and taunting you is even more fun than I ever imagined it would be."

"Taunting, heh! Now I'm afraid I'm going to have to show you a little trick Chip taught me, that is going to make you apologize for teasing me," Chris laughed.

"Oh, I don't think so," Surdas said, most assuredly.

"Thinking has nothing to do with it," Chris responded, as he started to tickle Surdas unmercifully.

"Stop! What are you crazy?" Surdas screamed, laughing as he succumbed to the torrent. "Of course thinking has nothing to do with it. You're doing it. Now Stop! Stop! You're going to make me pee myself."

"Apologize, little bro, or I'll have to rescue you from drowning in your own pee," Chris threatened.

"See! It's that hero complex again. Stop! Stop! I'm sorry! I'm sorry! I apologize!" Surdas surrendered.

"Not enough!" Chris teased, as he continued to tickle him. "Who's your favorite person in the whole world?"

"You are! You are! Now stop … please!"

As Chris stopped the onslaught, and basked in the glow of his victory, Surdas sat back up and said, "Oh Lord! Now I really have to pee. Are we almost wherever we're going, Auntie Allie?"

"Yes, but I'm pulling into the gas station up ahead, Sweetie," Aunt Allie said. "Just listening to you two tickles me. And I'm at an age when I really have to pee now too."

After the trio relieved themselves, they continued a little farther until they reached the khanqah, or Sufi lodge, where Uncle Mohammed and his fellow Sufis met. As they pulled up, Chris did his best to describe the building to Surdas in as much detail as possible.

"It sounds like something right out of *The Arabian Nights*," Surdas said, listening to Chris describe the architecture.

"That's exactly what it is," Aunt Allie smiled "and so is the experience you're about to have."

As Chris gave Surdas a hand to get out of the backseat, Surdas smiled and said, "You know I would have said that, even if you weren't tickling me."

"What? That you were sorry?" Chris asked.

"No! You dumb jock …" Surdas said as he punched Chris's shoulder, "that you're my favorite."

"I knew that, Brainiac. I just wanted to hear you say it again out loud. And just between us … you're mine too."

"But what about Molly? Isn't she your favorite?"

"That's a different favorite. It's a birds and the bees thing that you're too young to understand. You still haven't even figured out the aunts yet, never mind the birds and the bees."

When the trio got to the entrance, Chris was surprised to find Uncle Mohammed waiting there for them. "What's going on," he whispered to Aunt Allie. "I thought we were supposed to sneak upstairs and look over the balcony so that no one would know we were there."

"Well, it wouldn't do Surdas much good to look over the balcony, when he can't look over the balcony, now would it?" Aunt Allie replied.

"Will someone please tell me what's going on?" Surdas asked. "All I hear is a lot of whispering and some beautiful music in the background."

"I'll explain, Surdas," Uncle Mohammed said, stepping forward. "A while back, my brother brought Chris here to see my fellow Sufis and me during one of our ceremonies. Chris enjoyed it so much that my brother wanted to share the experience with you. As it wouldn't do you much good to watch quietly from the balcony as Chris was able to do, Ali asked if there was any way I could bring the experience to you. Would you like that?"

"I would love to find out more, Uncle," Surdas said, enthusiastically. "I have heard of the Dervishes who whirl, on NPR, but it is not something that I have a clear image or understanding of."

"Let's see if we can change that," Uncle Mohammed responded. "Shaykh Mustafa, who is Master of the Lodge, is traveling and cannot be here right now, but he has given me permission to show you, that which your eyes cannot see, yet you will now envision and know."

Uncle Mohammed took the boys inside, introduced them to the other members of the lodge, led them to the center of the room, and as he placed a camel's hair hat on both Surdas's and Chris's heads said, "This hat represents the tombstone of the ego."

He then dressed the boys in a black cloak and a wide white skirt, again describing what each article of clothing looked like to Surdas. "The white skirt represents the shroud of the ego, which will soon be lifted. When you remove the black cloak at the beginning of the Sama, or ceremony, it represents being spiritually reborn to the truth.

"The ceremony you're about to partake in is an intelligent and loving ascent to Perfection. By turning toward truth, you will grow through love, transcend the ego, meet and embrace the truth, and arrive at Perfection. You will then return as one who has reached maturity and completion, and is able to serve and love all of creation without discrimination. Are you ready to begin your journey?"

"I have never been more excited, Uncle," Surdas beamed.

"This is so much cooler than I ever expected," Chris added.

As the music started playing, Uncle Mohammed instructed the boys to remove their cloaks and experience their rebirth. He then helped Surdas to move his arms into a crosswise position, instructing Chris to do the same. "You now represent the number one," he said, "testifying to God's unity with all of creation." He then instructed them to open their arms and slowly start revolving from right to left around the heart while embracing all humanity with love.

"Begin slowly. Do not focus on your spinning. Focus on your journey toward truth. As you pick up the pace to the music, your right arm should be directed toward the sky to receive God's beneficence, and your left hand, in which direction you should be facing, should be pointed toward the earth as you spread God's beneficence to all living creatures. As your pace quickens to the music, your skirt will begin to flow, and your ego will be lifted, as will your thoughts on your spiritual journey. You will become one with the One Who Is All.

"Now go. Let the music and the chanting carry you. Meet the truth of your perfection … and His … and enjoy your most solemn meditation."

It took no time for the boys to become spiritually beautiful tops, spinning to feelings and emotions that they had never experienced before. It was a journey of a lifetime that lasted no more than a few minutes.

Since this was all new to Surdas and Chris, and they

were not accustomed to the type of whirling necessary for the ceremony, their meditation didn't last as long as a normal Sufi Sama. Still, by the time the music stopped, and their skirts ceased their magnificent whirl, both boys had a look of ecstasy on their face, and tears of joy in their eyes.

"I have never seen anything so beautiful in my life, Dear Uncles," Surdas remarked to the assemblage through an enlightened smile. "It is amazing how striking a vision can be, even without sight. This is an experience I will always cherish. I thank you all for making it possible."

"I would like to express the beauty you have given me in a more beautiful thank you," Chris added, solemnly, "but I cannot put into words all that I am feeling right now. So, from the tip of my tongue to the bottom of my heart … thank you!"

"You are both most welcome, my brothers, but there is much to be done here yet," Uncle Mohammed said, as he removed their ceremonial garb and escorted the guests out. "I'm truly glad that you have enjoyed your experience. If you wish to talk about it more, we can do so at another time. But for now, I must get back. I'll see you all at home later. And don't forget, you have my brother to thank for this."

As Uncle Mohammed disappeared back inside, the boys hugged Aunt Allie, and Chris said, "You're the best!"

"Thank you, Sweetie. It means a lot to me that you feel that way, but remember this is still our little secret; even the part about being 'the best.' No sense damaging anyone's ego. Like everything else, they become more fragile as we get older. Just remember to also give Uncle Mohammed a well-deserved hug later when he gets home."

"He looked so majestic today," Chris replied, "but I've never seen him look so serious … not even during martial arts practice."

"This is your uncle's first time leading the lodge," Aunt Allie smiled. "He has the weight of the whirl on his shoulders today."

The pun was not wasted on the boys, whose laughs nearly brought tears to Aunt Allie's eyes.

"You know, I can't tell you how much your enjoyment of our little outing means to me. I may not be the brightest bulb in the chandelier, but that doesn't prevent me from giving off a little light now and then. Just watching the way your faces lit up, did the same to my heart. You boys looked like the most beautiful spinning tops I've ever seen in my entire life," Aunt Allie beamed.

"Thank you!" they replied in unison.

"What's a spinning top?" Surdas whispered to Chris, as Aunt Allie walked around to the other side of the car.

"I'm not really sure," Chris shrugged. "Probably something from some old video game … or what will happen inside your head when I get to drive back home."

"Oh Lord!" Surdas moaned as he hopped into the back seat. "Wouldn't you know the first time I get to experience something heavenly, I'd wind up there?"

As they started out, Chris asked Aunt Allie if they were going to take the same route back home. "Of course, Sweetie," he answered. "Why do you ask?"

"I was just thinking that it may be fun to take the road less traveled," Chris answered, excitedly.

"That may not be such a great idea, Baby. "I don't even know who Les is, never mind the road he traveled."

Discretion being the better part of valor, Chris took the usual way home without further comment.

When they got back home, Mother asked Surdas where they had been all day.

"On a magical adventure, that took us to dangerous and mystical places," Surdas replied, "where lives were saved, wisdom was sought, and the truth was discovered."

Boys and their imaginations, Mother smiled to himself as Surdas made his way upstairs to his room. *I wonder where they were all day?*

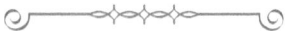

Fifteen

L ater that same evening, Surdas knocked on our bedroom door, to tell John and me about the non-secretive
part of his exciting day. But more importantly, I think, to
ask me a few questions about writing. He told me that,
since he enjoyed storytelling so much, he dreamed of
someday being an author. The problem was that he didn't
see how that would be possible, unless he dictated his entire story, and had someone else write it and bring it to
print.

He said that on more than one occasion, he convinced
Mother to read my stories about our family to him, and
loved them so much, that he convinced Uncle Josh to read
them to him a few times more.

"May I tell you something that I have been thinking
about for a while, Mr. Gene?" he asked.

"No titles, Surdas, remember? It's just Gene."

"OK, Just Gene," he smiled. "You are a great writer. I
feel as though I know every person's thoughts and every

person's heart in your stories. I would know them, even if I didn't know them. I want to be that kind of author too. I want my characters to become part of everyone's family. I want to bring laughter, and tears, and understanding to people's lives the way you do. Perhaps your shoes may be too big to fill, but someday I would like to at least follow in your footsteps.

"I have many stories in my head, outside of those which I've read and told. Like you, I would like to some-day bring them to print, and braille of course, so that I may find them with my hand, and not lose them off my lips. I'm just not sure of the best way to go about it. I was hoping that you might have some suggestions."

Flattery will get you almost anywhere, but a true passion will take you all the way. The next morning John and I took Surdas shopping for a new laptop computer with braille keyboard stickers on all the original keys, so that it became a bilingual keyboard, where he would recognize the keys, and I could read and help him with what he typed.

He was thrilled. He couldn't wait to begin. Since he had never used one, his first night practicing on the keyboard was a little frustrating, because he had to keep searching for the location of all the proper keys.

"I think there is a design flaw," he finally remarked. "Only I'm not sure if it's in the keyboard or me."

Actually, his frustration didn't last long. Over the next few nights, he quickly learned the entire keyboard and lap-top functions. He was every bit the whiz you would expect this little wizard to be. To make it easier for him to make corrections, and keep his writing to himself until he was ready to share it, I added a headset and an audio program that both audibly repeated the keystrokes and pronounced the finished word.

I attached a large separate monitor to his laptop so that I could assist him when needed. He needed the help less and less over the next few nights. Sometimes, as I watched the glow on his face as he typed away in front of the screen that was there for my benefit alone, I couldn't tell who was illuminating what. He seemed so happy. The funny thing is that John said the same thing about me whenever Surdas was with us.

"The way you guys beam when you're together is so amazing, that I practically have to put on sunglasses when I enter the room," he smiled.

"Take a look in the mirror, Diogenes," I returned the smile. "You'll admit to being quite the lamp yourself if you're an honest man."

The more Surdas and I worked together, the more John and I looked forward to his company. A night without Surdas was a night without sunshine.

"May I call you Uncle?" he asked, out of the clear blue sky, during one of our recent practice lessons. "I know that you are still young, but my respect and thankfulness is so deep that it would be an honor to do so."

"You may call me anything you like, Surdas," I smiled, "as long as you call me often, and call me a friend."

"You are truly that and more, Uncle," he said, as he hugged me. "You are my inspiration, my champion.

Thanks to you, someday I too will be a great writer. Someday, Bapu, I will make you proud of me."

"That day is already here, Buddy," I smiled, once again unconsciously allowing the Bapu remark to slip by. "The writing will just be icing on the cake. Now let's get to work and start racking up those Pulitzers. Tome and tide wait for no man."

Sixteen

Even though the boys' weekdays were school days filled with high school activities for Chris, and homeschooling with Mother and Uncle Josh for Surdas, Chris decided to make it his mission over the next couple of weeks to give Surdas as many boyhood adventures as he could squeeze into each day.

He took Surdas for rides through town on the handlebars of his bike, describing every detail that his eyes beheld, as though he was seeing them for the first time, which in some ways, he actually was.

The poet in Chris's soul was born, as he described trees that bent like old women picking up fallen branches, or their young saplings reaching for clouds, and the fruit their mother dangled above them. He humorously described the various people who looked like zoo and farm animals, and the various domestic animals that did them one better. He wove descriptions of scattered homes that looked like great masterpieces, and other master-less homes that looked like scattered pieces. There were dragons and castles all made of cloud, and the sounds of the boys' laughter, hardy and loud. There were people on leashes, and dogs that ran loose, and descriptions that sounded like Dr. Seuss.

OK! I got carried away, but you get Chris's drift. There was yet another beautiful thing happening inside of him. And, as in most beautiful things, it was borne out of love.

When he wasn't waxing poetic, Chris took Surdas on exaggerated adventures like exploring in an old cave that was no more than ten feet deep, but which he thought would seem like a much greater adventure to his blind buddy by the fourth time around. Chris even took the last trip around with his eyes closed so that he could experience it as much as possible the same way that Surdas did.

Remarkably, during that last tour, Chris stumbled and would have fallen had his blind buddy not had the foresight to catch him when he heard the stumble. Surdas smiled thinking that if Chris were truly blind, and not pretending to make the cave adventure seem much deeper, he would have remembered where that rock was by the third trip around.

Continuing their adventures, Chris also took Surdas on his first tree climb, describing the climb in such a way that had Surdas imagining they were out on a limb high above the treetops, although they were probably no more than a few feet above the ground. He took him fishing in a lake where they couldn't possibly catch any fish, using lines with no hooks for the safety of all creatures around, especially themselves. They went exploring for dangerous wild animals through a wood where there weren't any. He took him to a neighbor's barn where they could safely free fall from the hayloft into huge piles of hay. He took him skinny dipping in a part of the lake that was never deeper than Surdas's waist, where he could learn to trust the water.

That week, and every week thereafter, Chris took Surdas to all his soccer games. He took him to all the college football games that Robbie coached. He took Surdas everywhere he could think to take him, and in the end, Surdas was more than taken.

At each adventure, Chris would describe their quest as thrillingly and dangerously as possible, so that Surdas would imagine that he was on the most exciting, the most magical journey ever. Although Surdas secretly saw through much of the pretense, each day with Chris was exactly what Chris had intended, the most exciting, the most magical day of Surdas's life. Surdas's sole mate had become his soul mate. Chris had transformed a would-be Pinocchio into a real boy in the most magical of ways … just by pulling a few strings in his heart.

Surdas was a boy who never saw the sun, but every day, in every way, it rose for him every time he heard Chris's voice.

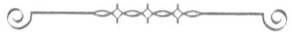

Seventeen

Robbie suggested, in keeping with Chris's Geppetto mission, that Chris, Molly, and Surdas could babysit Madeleine, so that all the adults could meet up with Chip and Dale in town to go to the movies. It was a suggestion appreciated by everyone, particularly Surdas, who was excited at yet another chance to spend some quality time with Chris and Molly. Besides, he loved playing with little Madeleine, who always managed to extract a new story out of him—usually one that Chris and Molly enjoyed as much as Madeleine, and many of which would eventually wind up in print.

As for the adults, we all met at Robbie and Mark's house to settle the babysitters in, and then pile into two cars for the short trip to the theater. Mother rode in the car with the aunts and uncles, and Dad rode with Robbie, Mark, John, and me. Dale, Lauren, and Chip were to meet us at the theater. When we arrived, Chip surprised everyone with his new date, Randy Cheung, a handsome fellow student and athlete of Chinese descent.

The introductions were going extremely well, until Randy moved toward me to shake my hand. Suddenly, Aunt Sue, who had remained behind in the car to primp for his entrance, let out a shriek from at least a block and a half away that was probably heard at least twenty blocks beyond.

"You're that Chinese boy, right?" Aunt Sue yelled rather sharply, while rushing toward us, and waving some object in front of him. "Our little League of Notions should have hunted you down the last time you literally became a pain in the ass. I have a hat pin that I carry around at all times that will match the prick of any prick that ever tries to mess with my family again."

A chorus of "Aunt Sue, please!" interrupted his remarks.

"This isn't Bryan, Aunt Sue!" I added quickly, referring to my past mistake. "It's Randy, no relation."

"Well how am I supposed to know? You must admit you Chinese boys all look a bit alike, with that same haircut and almond eyes and all. It's kind of like all those Southern folk with no branches on their family tree. But now that I'm up close, I can see that Chip has much better taste than Gene."

"Hey!" John and I both answered in unison.

"Sorry, Baby!" Aunt Sue said to John. "Present company was meant to be included."

"Wait! What?" John asked.

"I said I was sorry. Geez! Now I know Chip's rather

handsome Asian friend here may have had nothing to do with Bryan, but we all know the expressions about all the tease in China, and the best laid plans of vice in men that often go astray. So, you'll have to excuse me for throwing some wind at my caution. We've all been down this Silk Road before. That's all I'm saying."

"Sue, you make as much sense as change for a penny," Mother scowled.

"Well, aren't *you* one to coin a phrase," Aunt Sue laughed, mocking the expression. "I'm just saying that the last little wok on the wild side was with Bryan at Les Mis, the play, and now here we are at Les Mis, the movie, with another occident just waiting to happen. To my way of thinking, there is a fortune cookie full of coincidence staring us right in the face."

"Aunt Sue, do you know how prejudiced that sounds?" a more-than-shocked Chip pleaded.

"Oh please, Baby!" he replied. "Don't shoot the messenger. Let's get black to basics. I'm a Japanegro. Your little friend and I are skinfolks, give and take a few shades of separation. I'm only prejudiced if I pick on the whiter shades of pale."

"Is there anything I can say to ease that beautiful mind of yours?" Randy smiled, trying to melt the iceberg.

"Don't try to charm the pants off someone who isn't wearing any, Baby. This isn't an inquisition. I'm just inquisitive. I'm a killer aunt when it comes to protecting my family against anyone who tries to mess with them. So, while my hat pin is still out, I wouldn't mind hearing a thing or two about your good intentions."

"I assure you," Randy laughed, in a manner that was somehow as seductive as it was defensive, "as assuredly as you are certainly breathtaking, that my intentions are as good, as warm, and as inviting, regarding your nephew, as you could possibly want for him. I only intend on messing with Chip in the most pleasurable and satisfying of ways."

"Well now, I do like a like-minded spirit, to be sure," a relatively flattered and noticeably flustered Aunt Sue said, as he rapidly fanned himself. "I am certainly a fan of anyone who makes me do so. Is it hot out here, Baby, or is it just you? By the way, what did you say your name is again, Darlin'?"

"Randy," he replied.

"Randy!" Aunt Sue slyly pressed on. "Now I must admit that I'm more than excited to meet you, Randy. It's been a while since anyone has been able to get all my burners going. Are you sure that's your name, and not your attitude?"

"You know what they say," Randy smiled. "If the name fits … wear it. I try my best to wear it well."

"I must confess that I like the sound of your intercourse, Baby. And may I say, that not only the name, but the verbal Kama Sutra, suits ya as well. You've got my mind spinning all heels over head, if you know what I mean. You remind me of me when I was your age, a few short years ago."

And then turning to the rest of the group with a dismissive wave of his hand, Aunt Sue cut short the chorus, that surely was about to chime in, with a "No comments from the penis gallery. And that especially includes you girls … and by that I also mean you boys. This conversation has reached its climax and I'm already smoking."

"You'll have to excuse Sue," Mother said to Randy. "He's the larger-than-life ass in embarrass. Now put that silly pin away, Sue. You're like some crazy ninjcompoop."

"OK, everybody! Let's slither into the movie before this ceases to be almost totally embarrassing," Chip said, quite embarrassed. "And by the way, what the hell is the League of Notions?

"No, no, wait!" he interrupted Aunt Sue's intended response. "The questioner is dumber than the question for asking it. Let's leave it for another blushing experience."

"Smart move," I said, rubbing my younger brother's head as we entered the theater. "That college education is finally paying off."

"Yeah, but sometimes I think my legal degree should be in Murphy's Law," he admitted.

As we entered the theater, Dale, who was walking right behind John and me, asked Lauren what she thought of the sometimes-heated exchange.

"I thought that it was so hot that I can't imagine you're going to get any sleep tonight," Lauren gushed.

"I don't think Chip will either," Dale laughed. "And I don't even want to think about Aunt Sue."

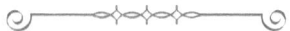

Eighteen

While the family was slithering and fanning their way into the movie theater, Molly, Chris, and Surdas were spending the evening playing kid games and telling stories with Madeleine. After they all grew tired, and Madeleine finally fell asleep, Molly, without thinking, asked Surdas if he'd like to see the video of the vampire movie that she and Chris saw on their first date.

"Will I be able to follow it without seeing all the action?" he asked sincerely, completely unaware of Molly's embarrassment at what she imagined to be a major faux pas.

"Of course you will," Chris rushed to her defense. "You'll have your play-by-play guy right here to explain everything that you'd need to see. That's the beauty of watching at home. Right, Molly?"

"Right," said Molly, who gave Chris a big rescue kiss.

"This is so exciting. I've never been to the movies," said Surdas. "And since I can't see the screen anyway, this is just as good. Too bad we don't have soda and popcorn."

"Who said we don't have soda and popcorn?" Chris smiled, as he rushed to the kitchen. "Three drinks and helpings of microwave popcorn coming right up! I'm pretty sure that we even have some candy to top it off."

An enchanted Surdas sat with a Cheshire Cat smile through the entire movie, as Chris described the action, and Molly added color commentary. "This is one of the finest nights of my life," Surdas volunteered, after the movie ended. "I never really imagined that I'd get to enjoy a movie like that, and with popcorn, no less. Thank you both. I can't tell you how much this means to me."

"It was our pleasure, Buddy," Chris offered. "We'll do it again soon, I promise."

"You are making me much too happy," Surdas beamed as all the soda began to kick in and he asked to be excused.

As Surdas got up to use the bathroom, Molly whispered to Chris, "We have to find some way to give him a real movie experience … movie popcorn, Raisinets … the whole deal."

"Maybe if we talk to the theater manager, he'll let us sit up in the balcony," Chris volunteered. "There's never anyone up there, so we won't disturb anyone if we're whispering all the action details to Surdas."

"We could take him with us tomorrow," Molly suggested.

"Are you kidding? It's a bloody, gory zombie movie," Chris said. "It's supposed to be one of the scariest movies ever made. It's perfect!"

Chris and Molly didn't discuss their plan with Surdas.

They wanted it to be a surprise. Soon after he returned to the living room where they were now watching a comedy rerun on TV, Surdas started to become drowsy and nodded off. He was, after all, only ten, had just experienced his first movie, and had gorged himself on popcorn, candy and soda. On a journey halfway through the hood between childhood and young adulthood, he surrendered to the peace and quiet of the more youthful neighborhood.

Chris knew that it would still be some time before the adults returned home, so he led the more-than-half-asleep Surdas up to his room and put him to bed. He was pretty sure Robbie and Mark wouldn't mind Surdas sleeping over, and he didn't mind bunking out on the couch for a night. Besides, it gave him more time alone with Molly, and that's always a good thing.

Nineteen

As Chris and Molly snuggled into the good time before them, the movie crowd was leaving the theater
discussing the good time they had just experienced. Since
only three of us had ever seen the play, we weren't allowed
any comparisons between the play and the movie. The
movie had to be judged strictly on its own merits. One by
one, Robbie, John, and I were excluded from the discussion for merely mentioning something about the play in
passing. Apparently, the rules were very strict.

The discussion on just how good the acting was grew
intense, and as Mother and Uncle Josh were lagging behind, putting the final stamp of approval on the movie,
Mother stopped in the middle of the street to pick up a
program of upcoming events that he dropped while making a point, and Uncle Josh continued walking. Mother
was distracted. He didn't see the car speeding toward him.
Everyone else in our group was distracted. We didn't see
the danger. The teenagers in the oncoming car were hors-

ing around. They were distracted. They didn't see the man stooping in the road ahead of them.

There was no honking, no screeching of brakes, nor any other sound to warn us. Before anyone realized what was happening, Mother was thrown spread-eagled on the ground, and the car sped past with its occupants never having seen the man that had been bending in front of them.

The aunts turned around a split second before the car passed, and were the only ones to witness what happened. They combined for a shriek of horror that would have made any banshee envious. Everyone turned to see the car speed by and Mother on the ground. We all panicked. Through a hail of screams and a flooding of tears, we rushed to Mother's aid expecting the worst. The chorus of "Oh My God!" and "Are you all right?" was deafening. We were all so frightened, and so relieved to see him sit up, that we scarcely noticed the large dog hovering over him.

"What happened?" Mother asked in a daze, as the dog licked a scratch on his face, and we helped him to his feet.

"I'll tell you what happened," Aunt Sue exclaimed, still panicked but unable to resist being a slice of over-cooked-ham performer. "Your train was ticketed for a trip to heaven, when this little angel here appeared out of nowhere, knocked you out of harm's way, and saved more than your caboose from being wrecked. If that baby didn't risk its life, you wouldn't have one. I don't think that car even saw you. You must have been bending in a way where they thought they were going through some sort of tunnel or something."

"Where did you come from, Sweetie?" Mother asked, still trying to shake off the scare, while contemplating wrapping his hands around Aunt Sue's neck for the tunnel comment. "You don't have a collar or any identification. Aren't you here with anyone?"

The dog walked over, jumped up, and licked another kiss to his face.

"I guess it is now," Aunt Sue chuckled. "That dog's here with you. I think you should call it Blackie."

"But he's red like your eyes, not black like the way I want to make them," Mother protested, still glaring.

"She's only red on the outside," Aunt Sue laughed. "But to get back to black, she has all the moves of a sleek black femme fatale, like the one who is speaking. But then again, since it's your guardian angel, I would say that she already came with a name ... Angel."

"So, you think it's a girl?" Mother asked, relaxing into the situation.

"You're a drag queen, Baby. Does it really matter? Although I don't see any telltale hints of masculinity around the area where there should be some telltale hints of masculinity. It's either a female, or the perfect drag dog."

"What type of dog do you supposed it is?" Mother wondered.

"It's a Doberman Pinscher," Uncle Josh volunteered.

"But it has floppy ears and a long tail like Sue."

"It's uncut," Uncle Josh added with a smirk, "definitely not Jewish."

"Whatever you are," Mother said to his young guardian

angel, "we can't leave my hero, or heroine, out here in the street. You're coming with us, till we find your home."

"Something tells me our little Angel already has," Aunt Sue whispered to Aunt Allie. "Ain't a living creature that ever walked into Mother's house that didn't walk out as part of the family."

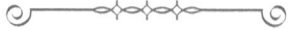

Twenty

When the still-shaken adults arrived at Robbie and Mark's home, my brother and Mark thanked Chris and Molly for babysitting, and took them both to drive Molly home. Dad, John, and I brought Angel to Dad and Mother's home, while Mother and Uncle Josh checked in on Surdas, who was sleeping in Chris's room.

He looked so happy and content that they didn't want to wake him, even though they wanted him to meet Angel. The prevailing thought was to let him sleep, but they were also a little concerned about the possibility of his waking up in a strange place in the middle of the night.

"Perhaps we should just let him be, and rely on the boy's natural abilities to understand his surroundings," Uncle Josh finally suggested, after seeing how serenely Surdas appeared to be sleeping. "This should be the only type of kid napping the world should ever know. Let him sleep in peace. There's not much we can do. It's not like it would do any good to leave a note, or even a light on."

"No! But one of those idea light bulbs just went on over my head," Mother said, as he called John and me to bring over the spare bed that Chris used when he slept in Chip's old room.

The four of us quietly set up the bed in Chris's room as Surdas slept, and when Chris returned with Robbie and Mark from dropping off Molly, Mother asked him if he would mind sleeping in the spare bed for Surdas's safety.

Chris, who was used to sleeping on the spare bed during sleepovers with Chip, thought it was a cool idea and readily agreed.

And sure enough, a few hours later, Mother's plan paid off. Surdas woke up in the middle of the night to use his bathroom which, of course, wasn't there. He drowsily walked into Chris's closet, rustled around, and then loudly exclaimed, "Oh Lord! I hope I'm dreaming! I think I'm trapped in some old locker room."

"Surdas," Chris called out, "are you OK?"

"Chris! What are you doing in my room?" Surdas asked, surprised.

"You're not in your room, you're in mine," he responded.

"Chris! What am I doing in your room?" Surdas laughed. "And why are all your clothes hanging in the bathroom?"

"You're not in the bathroom, you're in my closet. Don't go peeing in there until I have a chance to redirect you," Chris joked.

"Sure, now you tell me," Surdas returned the humor. "How do you flush a shoe tree, anyway?"

When Surdas returned from relieving himself in the proper facility, he asked Chris why he was still there.

"Well, you were pretty tired after the movie and all the junk food, so I brought you up here. When the adults came home, they thought you looked so comfortable that, rather than wake you, they thought we should do a sleepover."

"A sleepover? We're doing a sleepover? Why didn't you wake me?" Surdas asked, sincerely. "I could have slept through my first ever sleepover. That's practically like not ever having one. I could have missed the whole thing."

"Whoa! Whoa, Bronco! It's a sleepover. Believe it or not, the idea is to sleep."

"Not on your first sleepover," Surdas exclaimed. "And what's with the Bronco name?"

"I don't know," Chris said honestly. "It just slipped out."

"I like it," Surdas grinned. "I bet there aren't too many Indians with the nickname Bronco. Can I keep it?"

"I suppose so," Chris shrugged. "I don't think there are any rules on nicknames. But you should know that once they get started, they're hard to lose. The aunts still call me Cowboy."

"I know. It's so cool. I was afraid that they were going to start calling us Cowboy and Indian. Now we'll both have cowboy names, Bronco and Cowboy Chris."

"Cowboy Chris sounds like a Pixar cartoon. I'll call you Bronco sometimes if you just call me Chris. Deal?"

"Deal!" Surdas smiled. "See how much we've accomplished already on our sleepover. Imagine if we slept through it."

"I'm trying, Bronco," Chris laughed. "I'm trying."

"So, what should we talk about next?" Surdas asked, excitedly wide awake on the best night that Bronco Surdas could remember.

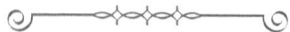

Twenty-One

Chris couldn't remember what they talked about next, but he did remember what he thought about next. It was an addition to their adventure repertoire that would benefit all involved.

He would ask Chip the next morning if it would be possible for the two boys to have a boys' night out/sleepover at Chip's apartment one night a month, after one of their soccer games. Chip had given him a standing offer that he had yet to accept. Perhaps just one night a month with the addition of Surdas wouldn't really be pushing it too far.

To no one's surprise, Chip's response was that it would be too difficult to decide which game night of the month would be best. So, since they played a game every week, they might have to expand the request to a weekly adventure, but only if it included pizza, soft drinks, and a monster or horror movie.

Chip's generous response twisted the happy place in Chris's heart far more than it had to twist his arm. It equated to four less sleepover possibilities for Randy, and even less of a possibility of sleep for Chip. But the joy and laughter of their boys' night out would sing in his heart from week to week, perhaps leaving him the happiest one of all. In the case of Chip's generosity, a thing of beauty is a boy forever.

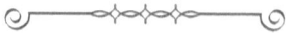

Twenty-Two

It's amazing how noticeably better things seem to get, as things get noticeably better. On the morning after the sleepover in Chris's room, as Surdas walked back into our house, he was surprisingly greeted by a huge lick to the back of his leg.

"Oh Lord!" he exclaimed. "That's too high a lick for little Hopi. Please tell me that it's not Mr. Chip trying to play another joke on me."

"This not-so-little angel rescued Mother from being hit by a car last night," I said, through the laughter at his remark, and placed Surdas's hand on top of Angel's head. "She's a red Doberman Pinscher. If she doesn't have a chip, and we can't find her owner, we may have a new addition to the family."

"Hi, Angel!" he said, as he fondly petted the dog's head. "If you saved Uncle Benji's life, you're everyone's guardian angel. Take it from me; life is good here. Ditch the chip if you have one."

As it turned out, Angel didn't have one, but she apparently had a new name and a new home. By late afternoon we were satisfied that there weren't any reports of a missing Doberman at any of the veterinarians or animal shelters. So, Angel joined Hopi as yet another queen, in a deck stacked with them.

Angel took to Mother the way Hopi took to Surdas. It was like they were soul mates. She would follow Mother everywhere he went, and seemed to understand his every word. Just as you would expect from an Angel, however, she shared her heart with every other member of the family as well. But in the end, her heart really belonged to Mother. And it's not hard to imagine how well that love was returned in kind. When unconditional love looks into a mirror it's usually a mother or a dog that looks out.

Twenty-Three

Later that evening, Chris and Molly were able to pull off their movie surprise. The manager of the theater was so touched by their thoughtful plan, he rewarded them with a jumbo-sized popcorn and soda as a complement, or per- haps compliment, to their generosity. Surdas was beside himself, and beside his buddy, Chris, all evening.

True to his promise, Chris whispered everything, from the previews, to the entire feature, in Surdas's receptive ear throughout the evening. A few loud "Oh No(s)!" slipped out of Surdas's mouth during the scary parts, but they couldn't be heard over the screams of the frightened teens below. Between the movie and the popcorn, soda, Raisi- nets, Milk Duds, assorted sour chews, and Chris, Surdas was figuratively and literally a kid in a candy shop.

Mark picked the kids up after the movie, and dropped Molly off at her home, before returning with the boys. I was still downstairs working in our house, when he and Chris dropped Surdas back home. Everyone else had gone to bed. I knew that Surdas would be excited about the experience, so I put everything aside when I heard him enter, and asked him about his night. Although he was animated and excited in his description of the evening, there was also a strangeness about his excitement.

"I can tell that something is troubling you, Buddy," I said. "What's up?"

"I'm not sure I should be talking about it, Uncle. It's confusing and kind of embarrassing," he said softly.

"I'm not Mother," I confessed, "but confusing and embarrassing situations are kind of my specialties, as I've lived through enough of them. Since we're friends, I want you to know that you can tell me anything."

"It's kind of about Chris," he responded, still unsure of himself.

"He's real important to you, isn't he?"

"I've never met anyone like him. He makes me feel so special, and yet so ordinary."

"I'm not really sure what you mean, Buddy."

"Most people treat me special because I'm blind," he began. "Chris treats my being blind the same way he would treat anyone else being short, or blond, or any other normal characteristic. He's never mentioned it … not once. It's not because he forgets that I am blind. It's because he remembers that I am more than blind. Even when I tease him about being blond or joke about my blindness, he never responds to my blindness, only to the humor. It's like my blindness is normal to him.

"Yet I know that he never ceases to protect and watch

out for me. He just does it in a way that he might do for someone who has sight but wasn't paying attention. Do you know what I mean?"

"I think so," I smiled. "Tell me more."

"When we are walking through the woods on the way to the lake, I can hear him lifting branches so that I won't bump into them, or kicking aside debris so that I won't trip. He never even mentions what he's doing. He just continues the conversation as though nothing is happening. If there is something in my path that is too large for him to remove, he'll jokingly give me a friendly shove that has nothing to do with the conversation, but everything to do with moving me out of the way of some sort of harm.

"He does the same thing when he's describing things to me. He never describes them as though I can't see them. He does it as though he's merely pointing them out, as though I just wasn't paying attention. So, you see, he makes me feel normal, like an able person, not a disabled one."

"First of all," I laughed, "never aspire to be just a normal person, especially not in front of Mother. You'll get another one of his famous lectures you weren't asking for. Besides, if anything, Buddy, you're supernormal, well beyond the range of normal. You're extraordinarily exceptional because you're extraordinarily you. Exceptional is determined by who you are, not what you are.

"Second, and most important of all, the friendship you guys share sounds perfect. I still don't see the problem."

"The problem is, suppose it's not just a friendship. How do I know if it's not more than that, and I don't like him more than that … like I'm, you know … gay?" Surdas asked, extremely seriously.

"Whoa! I have to admit I wasn't expecting that," I confessed, having been caught way off guard. "You're still pretty young."

Suddenly, I remembered that I was around the same age as Surdas when I first met Robbie. I remembered how that excitement felt; how confusing those feelings were. And I remembered the difficulties I experienced because I was too afraid to admit them to anyone but myself. Surdas was bravely taking the leap that I was afraid to take. I was determined not to let him fall.

"Not that it necessarily makes a difference that you're young," I added, quickly recovering. "It's not a question of age. But it is a question I can't answer for you. Only time and you can answer that question.

"But I can tell you this much … one way or another … you'll know. It will feel natural. It will be heartfelt. And it will feel right. You will know it is who and what you are, if it truly is who and what you are. And you will know it, whether you are true to it or not. Why do you ask?"

"Tonight, when Chris was whispering all the movie action in my ear, it felt so wonderful. It was so exciting to hear his voice, to feel his breath in my ear. I didn't want it to stop. It was the best part of the whole movie.

"Sometimes his lips would accidentally touch my ear, as he was whispering, and my whole body would shake with excitement. Then, towards the end of the movie, when he put his hand over my mouth to stop me from making too much noise when I got scared, I kissed it. I didn't mean to. It just felt so warm and exciting when he held it there. And then, it just happened. I don't know for sure if he even knows it.

"I was afraid after it was over, he would be upset or embarrassed, and I would have scared him away. But he didn't react at all. He just continued to describe the movie, and laughed and joked the rest of the night, as though nothing had changed. But maybe it did … at least in me. I still think about it. But I'm afraid of what *he'll* think about it."

"I really can't tell you what this all means, Buddy," I began, truly unsure of my footing, trying to guide this boy on a slippery slope. "I'm afraid you're going to have to figure this one out by yourself. Any assumption made by me, or anyone else outside of you, is just an opinion. The truth is yours alone. You'll have to decide whether this is the type of feeling someone has for a good friend, who really means a lot to them, or the type of feeling one has for someone very special, who means even more.

"Whatever you decide, you have to keep in mind, at least in this case, that the feelings you have for Chris, might be very different from the feelings he has for you. That doesn't mean that he loves you any less. But, if your feelings are romantic feelings, he probably loves you differently.

"Romantically, we both know Chris loves Molly. She's his girlfriend. She has been for quite some time now. It's safe to assume that he loves her differently than he loves you. But again, that doesn't mean he loves you any less. I have no doubt that you're his best male friend, and he loves you as such. But you have to remember, there is a big difference between having a boy as a friend, and having a boyfriend.

"I know that the distinction isn't as easy to concede as it sounds, when you're the one with the stronger feelings. I can tell you that I went through something very similar with Robbie, and Mother went through the same with Uncle Josh."

"I know. I've heard much about it," Surdas interrupted.

"Are there no secrets in this house?" I asked.

"Not that anyone's talking about," he half-heartedly smiled.

"Remind me to steal that line sometime," I continued. "It will work great in a story.

"Anyway, both Mother and I went through similar experiences when we were young. Neither of us was very smart about it. We ignored the truth staring us in the face, and focused on the mirror of our own feelings. That image was false, and we suffered for it … and so did the people we loved … through no fault of their own.

"It's never easy when your feelings are different from the other person's. So, you have to make it easy on yourself, and Chris, and meet where both your feelings are the same. Am I making any sense?"

"Yes, Uncle, but it's still confusing. I've never felt like this before. It would be so much easier if someone could just tell me what I'm feeling one way or the other."

"Someone will tell you what you're feeling, Buddy … the only one who can … *you* will."

"Thank you, Bapu," he said. "You have been most kind and helpful. I have much to think about."

"You're welcome, Buddy," I said, as unsure of my role in the conversation as I'm sure he was of his. "Get some sleep. You and Chris are good friends. I'm sure everything will seem fine in the morning."

"I hope so," he said, as he settled into a warm hug. "Goodnight."

I returned his goodnight with a kiss to the top of his head. As he started up to his room, I watched as some unseen part of me followed, still trying to comfort him.

I gave Surdas's question my best shot, my best Mother-like response. Yet, I felt even less like Mother, when he left looking as confused as when he entered. I truly wanted to be so much more for him, but I'm usually on the getting side of good advice, not the giving. My best shot, was a shot in the dark. I just hoped that it hit something, and that he found some light, in there somewhere.

I couldn't sleep at all that night. Surdas's digging for answers unearthed some questions and feelings that I had buried long ago. I more than understood his confusion: the solitary pain of longings and questions afraid to be spoken and asked aloud. I wanted to help, yet keep the trust of our private conversation. I tried to imagine what Mother would do. I decided against asking him, but I hoped he would have told me, I had already done it.

Twenty-Four

I wasn't sure if it was my place, but the next morning I sought out Chris, just to make sure there wasn't any strain in the boys' relationship. I found him mowing the lawn in front of his parents' house.

"Can I talk to you for a minute, Buddy?" I asked, as I interrupted his mowing and plugged-in musical accompaniment.

"Sure," he responded, as he unplugged himself from the tinny earphone remnants of some sounds I've never heard before. "What's up?"

"Surdas told me he had a great time with you and Molly last night, but he seemed a little anxious about something when he got home. I was just wondering if everything was OK with you guys."

"Sure! Of course! There's no problem. We had a great time. He's a great kid! He's like a best friend and brother all wrapped into one.

"He did seem a little quiet towards the end though. I

hope he's not upset that I covered his mouth when he was getting loud, or embarrassed that he kissed my hand when I did it."

"So, you know that happened?"

"You mean the kiss? Yeah! It was no big deal. I think that he just got caught up in the excitement of everything, and did what any kid might do. You know … kind of a big brother, little brother thing. We're pretty close."

"So, you're OK with everything?"

"Are you kidding? Why wouldn't I be OK? That little kid is one of the best things that ever happened to me. He makes me feel special … like some sort of hero or something. Plus, he's really smart and funny, and fun to be with. He's like some old guy with a great sense of humor, crammed into a little whiny kid. I have the best time with him. And I really miss him when he's not around.

"I hope he's not upset, or worried, or anything, because I'm not. To tell you the truth, I can't even imagine he could ever do anything that would change the way I feel about him."

"You're a pretty amazing kid, yourself," I said, patting him on the back. "You really are some sort of hero."

"See, it's catching," he laughed. "Wanna kiss my hand?"

In some ways I truly wanted to. This boy could not have been any more Robbie's son, if Robbie had actually given birth to him. I resolved to keep a hands-off attitude, knowing that Surdas's best interests were securely resting best in Chris's, already been kissed, hands. Apparently not every silver lining has a dark cloud.

"I can't begin to tell you how proud we all are of you," I added. "Your eyes and your heart have become the windows to two people's souls, and they're both the more beautiful because of it."

"Thanks, I guess," Chris shrugged. "Do you think that maybe we could be a little less poetic? I'm not really sure I'm getting where you're going with this."

"I'm sorry, Buddy! I'm just trying to say, that Surdas's world is so much happier when he sees it through your eyes. Everything you describe to him makes his world that much richer, that much more alive. It's the beauty he sees in you, that allows him to see the beauty that you are describing."

"I wish that was the case," he sadly smiled. "The amazing thing is, that it's actually the other way around. It's me seeing the world through Surdas and his eyes."

"What do you mean?" I asked, as I watched his eyes begin to water.

"He's such a great kid! I want so much for him. I want him to know and feel everything. When I see anything that's really special, like some big, majestic tree, or something, it kills me that he can't see it. It's so unfair. And what kills me even more, is that I probably wouldn't have seen it either, if I weren't trying to describe things to him … if I didn't want him to see it. Without him, I probably would have passed it by, never noticing that it was there, and how beautiful it was.

"If it wasn't for his eyes' inability to see, mine would

never have seen that tree, or anything else like it. And we would both be poorer for it.

"Sometimes, when we are walking through places like the little park in Town Centre, I look at the trees and bushes, the grass and flowers, the two little fountains, the ducks in the pond, and the birds, the bees and the butterflies floating by, and I wonder how I could possibly describe these things to him in a way that he could understand. He has never seen anything floating on the water, or floating in the air. He has never seen shapes or colors, sizes or patterns. What images come to his mind, if any, at my descriptions?

"When I describe the things that I see in the park to him, I watch his face, as he tries to puzzle it all together, and I start to cry. I can't help it. How can he possibly picture and understand something he's never seen? How can I possibly offer him anything except more confusion?

"I know he knows my tears, but we both pretend they aren't there, even though they almost always are. It's so frustrating that I can't give him what I see. I can't give him the best. All I can give him is my best, and hope that it's better than nothing."

"Hey," I smiled, as I took the liberty to wipe away one of his tears. "Who's waxing poetic now?"

"He does that to me," he confessed, almost sobbing. "He makes me more creative, even poetic. That's what I mean. That's what I'm trying to say. He makes me a better person. He helps me to see and understand things that I never did before. It's amazing how little you see when you can, and how much you can see when you can't. So, you tell me … who's helping who … who's the hero?"

"Thanks, Buddy! You've taught me a lot," I said, as I hugged him and started to walk away. "Just remember, you're both heroes, to each other, and to the rest of us. You have no idea how much better you both have made all our lives."

"Hey! If you're talking heroes, don't leave yourself out," he called after me. "You're a huge hero to Surdas, actually to everybody, but especially to him. He loves you and John, more than you can imagine. He loves Mother and Dad, but you guys are the parents he's always wanted. He's told me that. He just doesn't know how to tell you guys."

Those words cut through me like the sharpest of knives. It turns out, Surdas felt the same way about us, as John and I felt about him. Chris's words would have been the most beautiful I ever heard, if it weren't for the fact that our feelings were a complicated secret, considering that it was my parents who were fostering the boy.

Chris must have somehow sensed my reaction and concerns, and called out further, "It's pretty messy for him too. He loves this family. But I feel you should know; he especially loves you guys. That's where his family begins."

"Thanks!" I cried, as I felt the tears swelling in my eyes, and I ran back to hug him again.

"I told him you felt the same," Chris smiled, as he returned the hug. "I know you do. I just hope that someday soon you can tell him too. He's still a kid. Kids need to hear these things. I know it will mean the world to him."

"Me, too!" I said, as I dried my eyes. "It will mean the world to me, too." And this time I took his hand, and kissed it.

"See?" he laughed, as I walked away.

"Yeah! I do," I said. "I really do."

Twenty-Five

I could tell by Surdas's demeanor over the next couple of days that nothing had changed in his relationship with Chris, and he was able to relax back into their normal routine. Although he didn't broach the subject of his sexuality, or the kiss again, he began to seek me out for other conversations multiple times a day. Sometimes it was merely to talk, but most times it was to learn more about the art of the written word.

At just about every meal we shared together over the next few weeks, Surdas would ask me all sorts of questions about writing, style, and punctuation. Every time I asked him what he was working on that had him so intent, he would say, "You'll see, Uncle. It's a surprise."

A month to the day from when he started his writing, the little magician handed me his first written story ever.

"This is my gift to you, Uncle," he said. "It's a fable about a person who has your heart, who knows your art."

Twenty-Six

IF EVER A WIZ THERE WAS
By Surdas
(Age 10)

There are all types of magic in this world. Sometimes, the most magical doesn't involve magic at all. It involves something much simpler, something that is magic in its own right.

Jean didn't know magic. He didn't even like magic. He would never think of practicing it. He was too busy practicing something he held in higher esteem; he was too busy practicing love.

Jean came from a long line of magicians. His forefathers were both famous and notorious for their practices. Not that any of them were evil in any sense of the word. They made it a practice to only use their practice for the betterment of others. But there is a respect, deeply rooted in fear, which comes from a deliberate show of power. Jean's forefathers enjoyed that power, and loved the respect.

Jean was very different. He didn't want anyone to fear him. He had no use for power. And he did not understand a respect that wasn't mutual. He met everyone on the same level, and did his best to help elevate anyone who somehow felt they were below him. He helped them to realize there was never a time when they weren't equal, when everyone wasn't equal.

Without ever realizing it, Jean was practicing the most powerful magic of all. He was practicing the magic of wisdom. He was practicing the magic of the heart. For all practical purposes, however, Jean wasn't doing anything more than just being Jean.

Jean's father, the Master Magician, was upset, and thought that Jean was being foolish in not practicing the art that he was born into. Magic was prestige. Magic was tradition. By Jean turning his back on all that his father could teach him, the Master felt that Jean was not only insulting him, but also the entire family tradition. The Master would not hear of this. This was more than he could tolerate.

One day, the Master Magician decided to teach Jean a lesson, by putting on a spectacular and fearful display of power, in order to frighten some sense into Jean, and demonstrate how awesome the practice could be. The demons and specters he summoned were enough to frighten the life out of any mortal. Their terrifying approach to Jean's home could be heard for miles around.

Jean heard their advance, but it was not their terror that he sensed, but rather their pain. Jean knew that only a tortured soul could make those sounds, could sound that frightening.

When the fearsome horde arrived at his doorstep, Jean greeted them with the same love, compassion, and understanding, with which he greeted all of creation. He welcomed them into his home; greeted them with kindness and understanding; and refreshed and nourished them with his compassion and thoughtfulness.

The frightful visitors were stunned by Jean's kindness and generosity. They had never experienced anything like that. They felt something wonderfully strange overtaking them. It was warm and beautiful. They felt themselves being transformed. They became happy, even joyful, and immediately began to take on forms of enchantment, enchantments that delighted everyone they subsequently encountered.

The appearances and demeanors of the once-frightening horde changed so dramatically, and became so fair and inviting, that everyone began to refer to them as the Fair Folk, or Fairies.

Flustered, the Master Magician tried again. This time he cast a spell of greed and desire on Jean. Surely the hunger for all that he could have, would make him understand the power of his gift. The spell seeped into Jean's room as he slept. He felt it trying to take hold of him. He realized it was trying to play tricks with his mind. It showed him visions of wealth and power that were beyond belief. It whispered pleasures that even the most temperate of men would succumb to.

Jean knew a trick when he saw one. He didn't believe any of it. He didn't succumb. He knew better. He knew all too well the trappings of wealth and power. He thoughtfully sprung the traps, carefully preventing them from ensnaring him. And then he surrounded the vision with a trap of his own … a desire to share the wealth and power of kindness with everyone, and the pleasure of being a force for good.

Having once again recast the spells of the Master, Jean strolled into town as usual, where he helped the needy, visited the sick and elderly, dispensed smiles where they were needed, offered a hand where it was appreciated, and eventually returned home in peace. And the only spell that was affecting him, was the satisfying one of another day well spent.

The Master Magician was more than flustered. He could not understand the failure of his magic. This had never happened before. He decided to go into town as Jean had done, to see if the people there could give him a better understanding of why his own magic did not work on Jean and, more importantly, why Jean would not practice it.

The Magician visited the needy, who could not understand his question, because Jean always gave so much of himself and all he possessed, that they never felt needy after he left. No one's eyes had ever seen through their need the way his did. No one had ever enriched them as much as he had. Was that not magic?

He visited the sick and elderly, who were equally confused by his question, because they felt so much better after each one of Jean's visits, that they would forget they were sick or old. No one's words had ever healed them as well. No one's ears had ever heard them so clearly. Surely that's magic.

Then he spoke to the people in the streets, who were also confused, because Jean's smile was so magical, that he always uplifted their spirits. No one else could lift the heaviness of life the way he did with a simple smile. Is there any magic more powerful?

And finally, he spoke to the people to whom Jean had lent a helping hand, who, in turn, asked him what was more magical than helping someone who truly needs it, while asking nothing in return?

The Master Magician was in shock. He had been wrong all along. He realized Jean's magic was far more potent than his own. Jean was an accomplished magician. He was a true wizard. True wizards do not need magic. They *are* magic. There is magic in everything they do. Their magic emanates from how they see; from what they hear; from what they do; but mostly, from how they love. Jean's magic came not from a wand, or a potion, or a spell, but from the heart. It was the most powerful magic of all.

If ever a wiz there was, Jean was.

Twenty-Seven

The little magician's story brought tears to my eyes, by elevating my status to his, simply because of an act of kindness, and a shared interest in storytelling. It was an honor I had not come close to earning. I knew I was not nearly the magician imagined by this young boy, but I promised myself that I would do my best to be the person he imagined me to be.

At age ten, Surdas was already a better writer than I was when I started writing at two years his senior, and in some ways better than I am now. It makes sense. If he could easily captivate an audience with his take on someone else's writing, imagine what he could do when he honed his own.

I compounded my promise to mirror Surdas's image of me, to include doing anything and everything I could, to help him become the great writer he wanted to be—the writer he was rapidly becoming.

To that end, we formed a two-person writing club

that met twice a week to discuss creative ideas, and practice various writing techniques, ranging from ad-libs, to poetry, to prose. Each week he would floor me with the height and breadth of his creativity. In my attempt to mentor him, he made me a better writer. We were becoming so close, and spending so much time together, that John started, for the first time, to voice our secret desire—to refer to him as our son … but only in private. We had no intention of fostering any bad feelings by stepping on my parents' fostering toes.

Twenty-Eight

My second book was finally published the first week in October, and my publisher summoned me back to New York City for the launch and several book readings and signings at some of the major bookstores. The launch was scheduled for a Friday night, with additional readings and signings spread throughout the following week. John was unable to join me for the first weekend of the trip, because of his duties as minister, but agreed to be there for the weekdays following. I was prepared to spend that first weekend alone, when Chip came up with a better plan.

Chris and Surdas were scheduled for a boys' weekend at Chip's apartment. Since neither Chris nor Surdas knew much of the City, and since it would certainly be more exciting to be there than Chip's apartment in town, Chip suggested that they all come and keep me company for the weekend, and lend their support at the launch and book signings. It was too good a deal to pass up, and it would give me the opportunity to act as a guide, in perhaps the world's greatest city. I was all over it. We were going to experience one of those experiences of a lifetime.

We boarded our train to Manhattan early Friday morning, and it would probably have been a less than uneventful experience, were it not for the two boys sitting opposite one another in the window seats. As the train left the station, Chris immediately began describing the scenery to Surdas in such beautifully humorous ways, that Chip and I immediately became an unwitting audience for the entire trip. Sometimes, I would close my eyes to try to envision how Surdas was imagining Chris's clever descriptions.

There were the little towns that looked like the zombie apocalypse had already passed through. There was the mysterious vampire lady, standing in the shadows on one of the platforms, next to a bench covered with the disheveled remains of what must have been one of her victims. There was a high school band practicing in a school yard that didn't need a humorous description, because they marched to the music, and the music spoke for itself … in tongues. There was the ghost town where no one could possibly live in … at least alive, and the goat town where everyone, including the ladies, had beards. There was a sign that said, "Pee skill High School" because the k in Peekskill had been carefully blotted out. There were two boats on the Hudson River that looked like Chinese junks, only as in yards, not ships. There were even a few tugboats, some of them sunbathing on the front of their yachts. Add these, and a dozen or so more of Chris's descriptions, to the conductor who sounded like he was crying out, "All are bored." at every stop, and it added up to an extremely amusing trip.

We arrived in the City by mid-afternoon, with just enough time to grab a few slices of the famous Artichoke Basille's Pizza on 14th Street, run over to our apartment in Chelsea, shower, change, and dash to the book launch a few blocks away, but not without stopping for a few street hot dogs along the way. This was to be, after all, a New York experience.

My agent did a fantastic job arranging the launch. He managed to get enough publicity to fill the loft where the launch was held, and have a *New York Times* reporter on hand to write about it. All the food and refreshments were sponsored by local establishments that were more than happy to advertise their products at a well-attended event. And there were even a few local literary celebrities on hand to lend color and credibility to the event. On a scale of 1 to 10, with Chip and the boys by my side, it was a 99. I deducted one point for the wine that one of the overly wined celebrities spilled on a box of my books. After the event, we called it a night … an absolutely spectacular night. We returned to the apartment, settled sleeping arrangements, and allowed Morpheus to guide us through what little remained of the day.

There was nothing scheduled the following day until 8 p.m., so we had most of Saturday to explore the City. We started with cream cheese, lox and bagels for breakfast just down the street, and then we were off to the subway and onto our adventure.

We started in Times Square, where even Chris had a hard time describing the sites to Surdas. *If it's hard to describe it in the morning*, I thought, *just wait till he sees it at night.* As much as I couldn't wait to hear that description, somehow I knew Chris would be on it.

From Times Square, we headed over to Rockefeller Center, where the boys surprised me by agreeing to try something they had never attempted before … ice skating, at one of the world's most public venues no less. Chip agreed to show Chris the ropes, while I helped guide Surdas around the rink.

It's funny how these things sometimes work out. Chris, who is quite the athlete, and who thought skating would be somewhat of a breeze, was skating more like he was caught in the middle of a tornado. He never fell, which was a shame, because a fall might have looked much more graceful than all his attempts not to. Surdas, on the other hand, took to the ice immediately, and only needed guidance as far as traffic and direction around the rink.

"I guess I was so used to skating on thin ice with the sighted kids at the home," he laughed, "that it's easier to glide on a less slippery slope."

When he asked me how Chris was doing, I told him that Chris looked more like he was breakdancing than ice skating.

"Well at least now he can dance," he laughed again. "Mother told me Chris dances like the karate skid. I can't even imagine what it must look like, and yet you can be sure that I will be playing the scene over and over again in my mind for the rest of our trip."

When we finished skating and were returning to our civilian footwear, an older woman who had been watching us skate, commented that I must be very proud of my son for overcoming his handicap.

"Actually, the only handicap he has, is skating with me," I smiled.

But before I could even think about correcting her on our relationship, Surdas added, "My father and I are very proud of each other. I am only handicapped when we are apart."

His words wrapped around me like a warm comforter on a cold night. I knew from my conversation with Chris, he wasn't just being polite. I knew that he knew that I felt the same way. Perhaps, even more than Surdas, I was the one who was handicapped when we were apart. He was not my flesh, but he had more than gotten under my skin.

We were all starving after skating, so it was time for another unique New York experience … pastrami and corned beef sandwiches at Katz's Delicatessen, with meat piled so high, you practically have to climb on top of them to start eating. It's hard not to overdo it at Katz's, so we took the easy way out, and didn't even try, by also ordering the franks, the knishes, and the latkes, to go along with two rounds of egg cream sodas. An hour and a half later, we waddled our way up to Greenwich Village to shop for some supplies for the apartment, and then made our way back home to get ready for the evening's reading and book signing.

The venue for that night's reading was much simpler than the night before. It was just a bookstore without elaborate celebrity fare and refreshments. I was worried Chip and the boys might find the event a bit boring without all the accoutrements, but they truly seemed to enjoy it. They probably didn't enjoy it as much as I enjoyed having them there, but they seemed quite happy just the same.

After the reading and signings, we made our way back down to Bleecker Street, to Cones ice cream shop, for corn ice cream with cinnamon liberally sprinkled on the scoops. There is an ice cream heaven, and we were in it. We all double scooped, and then actually took a few pints home with us, in case any sweet dreams needed an enhancement during the night. Apparently, Chris's and Surdas's did.

Before I knew it, it was Sunday morning, our last full day together, since the visiting trio was scheduled to return upstate the next afternoon. So we decided to cram in as many big city activities as we could before they left. After a quick breakfast of eggs and bagels—of course New York is all about the bagels—we took the subway up to Central Park. After a stroll through Strawberry Fields, and lying on the grass of The Great Lawn, we made our way over to Lincoln Center, and then back down to Times Square, where we took our chances at entering the lottery for tickets to the matinee performance of *Wicked*. Chip and Chris both won two tickets each, and the four of us got front-row seats. I'm not sure which set of boys was more excited, but Chip and I were as much kids in a candy shop as the other two, who filled up at a real one, right before the show.

After the theater, it was off to Junior's Restaurant for dinner and, of course, cheesecake. Then, it was on to as many of Times Square's PG eye candy and real candy tourist traps as the boys could handle. And yes, I mean the big boys too.

In case you were wondering, Chris's description of The Great White Way at night ran something like, "It looks like you filled yourself with all the sugar and candy that your body can take, and then put your finger in an electrical outlet." Chip and I were a little perplexed at the vision, but Surdas excitedly responded, "COOL!"

After all the magic of the night, Surdas rubbed his lamp for a little more, and asked if there was any possible way they could stay for the rest of the week. "When you're flying high with the angels, why would you want to leave heaven?" he asked.

The problem was, Chip had work that he couldn't escape, and Chris had classes, soccer practice, and a game, that he had to get back for. But as for Surdas, a quick call to Mother revealed that he was way ahead in his homeschooling, and could easily miss the week, if the soon-to-be-visiting John and I were up for it.

I'm sure I was happier at the prospect than Surdas was. We would miss our weekend partners, but John would do much to even the change in dynamics. And so, with heavy, yet joyful hearts, we saw our companions off at the train station the next afternoon, and set out for a PG version of a night on the town, before John's arrival the next morning.

As we boarded the subway for the trip back downtown, Surdas suddenly hugged me, and said, "I am so happy we will have this time together. I can't tell you how much it means to me. I truly mean it when I say you are my hero, and nobody means more to me."

"You mean the world to me too, Surdas … more than you'll ever know," I found myself responding, still not knowing how to tell the boy just how much he meant to me. Stunned by my inadequacy, I admitted, "And I appreciate the sentiment. But I must confess that I'm not exactly what anyone would call a hero."

"Time has a way of making everyone Person of the Year," he smiled knowingly. "You just have to seize the right issue."

"Where do you get these lines from?" I asked in amazement. "That's positively brilliant. If you don't use it, I'm going to steal it."

"How can I tell you where something comes from, when it was always there?" he shrugged. "The important thing is … where are we going to eat?"

"How does the best Indian food in New York sound to you?"

"Like I haven't died and gone to heaven," he smiled.

"I'd say I'm going to use that line sometime … if I hadn't done so already," I said, jokingly.

"Hey, I often quote my favorite authors," he laughed. "They make me sound very wise and creative."

So, off my little creative wise guy and I went to Tamarind Tribeca, where our host was so taken by my young companion, that he offered to show him the best seat in the house.

"I'm afraid that your gracious offer is a bit wasted on me," Surdas replied politely. "But my good father here has lovingly ushered me around your beautiful city, as though I was some sort of prince. The father of a prince deserves nothing less than your finest table. So, if you please, kind sir, allow him the honor of your offer."

"Does he always talk like this?" our host asked, in amazement.

"Except when he's sleeping," I laughed. "Then he actually talks a little more like a ten-year-old boy … in between the snoring."

Our host showed us to a wonderful table, helped us order an exquisite meal, and offered us complimentary glasses of his finest mango latte. As we sat there, thoroughly enjoying our time together, I kept thinking how Surdas often referred to me as his father. And, for the first time in my life, I felt like one, the father of a prince no less. And though I knew in my heart it was not a wish that I should be wishing, I confess that I desperately wished it were so.

Twenty-Nine

The next morning, Surdas and I found our way back to the train station to pick up John. We grabbed a quick bite in the station, so that Surdas could have us send a picture and text to Chris of us eating at the bagel kiosk where he and Robbie first met. Then we ran back to the apartment to drop off John's luggage before setting out on another adventure.

Tuesday in New York City is one of the slower days, which means there was still more to do than you could possibly imagine. Chinatown and Little Italy seemed like a great start, and so we started there. We walked through all the shops with John and I on "Chris detail," describing anything and everything we could lay our eyes or Surdas's hands on. We bought all sorts of souvenirs, including lucky Buddhas, New York T-shirts, and Yankee baseball caps. Whatever we bought, Surdas made sure that we also bought one for Chris, so that he wouldn't feel so bad about not being with us. After strolling around for a few hours, and loading up on souvenirs, it was off to The Peking Duck House for a meal of its namesake dish, followed by an overkill of green tea, lychee nut, and mango ice cream at the Chinatown Ice Cream Factory.

By late evening, we were back in the apartment for a quiet night at home. It was so peaceful, that none of us lasted more than an hour, and all of us slept through the night. Maybe the City doesn't sleep, but sometimes, you just have to.

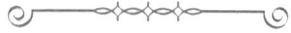

Thirty

The next afternoon, I was one of two writers who were doing readings and book signings at a major midtown bookstore. There were rumors the event might be picketed by some of the loonies from an anti-gay church, because both of us had taken pot shots in our books at the church and its leaders. We were told some sort of *Looney Tunes* confrontation was inevitable. After all, we were gay, and they were, well, loonies, marching, or at least picketing, to the peculiar beat of their own conundrum.

I didn't want Surdas to come to the event, because I didn't want him exposed to the hateful tirades of these Tiraders of the Lost Ark. Surdas insisted that he come, however, since he obviously wouldn't be reading their hateful signs, and knew all about them anyway. John, who would have stayed behind with Surdas, had he not come, agreed that I would fare much better with their moral support. Apparently, the only "No" they would accept had to do with my getting my way. In my family, my way is usually way out of the way, anyway.

Sure enough, when we got to the bookstore, there were a half dozen protesters, armed to the teeth with their hateful placards. There were twice as many placards as protesters, and probably twice as many protesters as brain cells, so I'm really not sure who was outnumbered. But, as you can probably imagine, I was relieved that I didn't get my way, and had my brilliant posse by my side.

We stopped a few feet short of the protesters to discuss strategy with the bookstore's event organizer. She was sure they wouldn't recognize me as one of the authors, but thought, for Surdas's sake, it would be better if John and I entered the store not looking like a couple. We weren't thrilled with the idea of surrendering anything of ourselves to the motley crew, but considered it prudent to be discussing defense, when everything offensive was on the other side. As it turned out, it didn't matter much anyway.

As the organizer was proposing tactics, we failed to notice that Surdas had quietly slipped away, and courageously headed directly toward the protest. He blindly followed the sound of their hateful spew, armed with more foresight than they will ever see.

"Excuse me," he said, as he walked directly into one of the placards, "what does this sign say?"

"Why don't you ask one of your parents?" the woman carrying the sign replied. "Can't you read?"

"I wear my sunglasses at night, because I am blind," Surdas countered, "and my birth parents are, unfortunately, dead, making it extremely difficult to ask them. So, please tell me what the sign says."

"Why don't you ask someone else?" she said, either embarrassed or uncomfortable with the situation.

"I don't understand! Are you ashamed of your own sign?" he countered again.

"Of course not," she replied, obviously lying.

"Then surely you should have no problem reading it to a ten-year-old child," Surdas smiled.

"It says, 'God hates fags,'" she said, in a low voice.

"And this one?" Surdas asked, feeling his way over to the sign next to her. "What does this one say?"

"It says, 'All fags burn in hell!'" she replied.

"So, this god you speak of, appears to be a very hateful god," he responded. "He must be very evil."

"Of course He's not evil!" she answered vehemently. "He just hates fags, because they go against his rules."

"So, I guess he doesn't have any of those 'created in His own image', and 'love one another', rules."

"Those rules don't apply to homos. God didn't create any homos."

"So, since everything is created by someone," Surdas continued, "the homos must have been created by a better god, with better rules, since neither their god, nor his creations hate the way yours does.

"It makes sense when you think about it. No god worth following would make hateful rules against his own creations. The homos, therefore, must have been created by a more loving god than yours. Perhaps you should shop around for a better god."

"There are no other gods," she replied. "There is only The One who created everything."

"So, you're saying that the god who created everything, hates his own children, his own creations?" Surdas persisted. "He must either be a terribly fickle parent, or a pretty lousy creator."

"Who are you? And what are you trying to pull?" the woman angrily asked, as the rest of the loonies in the bin gathered around to listen intently. "Is this some sort of joke?"

"I doubt if anyone is laughing," Surdas countered. "And, it is certainly not a joke on my part. I'm not the one out here carrying ridiculous signs, and saying horrible things, that make absolutely no sense, in the name of a god, who is obviously hateful. Perhaps you should find a more loving god, like the ones that teach about love and not judging others—you know, the ones the good religions have. Then, maybe you can say helpful things to others that make them feel good about themselves, instead of making everyone angry and upset.

"You'll have to excuse me for saying this, but your god sounds more like one of those hell creatures that turn all their minions into detestable demons. If you go to join him after you die, I am sure that you will see firsthand, it isn't the fags who will be burning in hell."

"Maybe you should go to hell," the woman shouted, obviously frustrated.

"I'm not sure if that is an invitation to join your religion," Surdas said, politely, "or simply a plea to understand your life? In either case, I think you need help. Please get it. A mind may be a terrible thing to waste, but to waste a heart, is truly a sin. As I see it, and I mean that figuratively of course, you are wasting both. Therefore, you are wasting a life, and that is probably the most horrible of all your sins."

Surdas was visibly startled, when a huge round of applause broke out behind him. At least two dozen people had stopped to witness the exchange that had everyone, including John and me, mesmerized. Surdas was the hero of everyone in the crowd who had ever felt the sting of ignorance and hate. We waited for all his newfound fans to finish congratulating him before escorting him into the bookstore. As we did so, an elderly gentleman stayed behind, and addressed the female protester.

"I hope that you realize by now, that you have it all wrong, Young Lady," he insisted. "You have an 'F' on your sign where an 'H' should be. God doesn't hate fags. He hates hags, vicious and malicious women, and men for that matter, although I doubt there are any real men among your group."

"Actually, I'm wrong," he corrected himself. "God doesn't really hate anyone, not even hags like you, and certainly not people who have the courage to love each other in the face of hate, like yours. But until you learn that, until you find the courage that is borne of real love, you should probably correct your sign to say, 'God even forgives hags', and hang it in your bedroom. God willing, maybe someday you'll wise up to become the type of intelligent human being that young man is."

Best book signing ever!

Thirty-One

The readings and signings went well. The protestors departed soon after their scolding. The encounter drew most of the witnesses inside the bookstore, and both authors sold more books than we anticipated. We credited that to the Surdas effect. A few people even asked him to sign their books as well.

As we gathered our belongings, and were preparing to leave the bookstore, John pointed out a furry bison toy near the store's exit.

"I bet it looks just like Biff in your first book," Surdas said to me, excitedly, referring to my early story about a young bison. "May I feel him? I've always wondered what a bison like Biff felt like."

"You remember that story?" I asked, quite flattered.

"I can probably recite it to you verbatim," he smiled, petting the toy as though it were a much-loved pet. "It's my favorite … or at least one of them."

"Well then, I think this Biff needs a new home," I laughed.

"I think you are going to make me cry like some little kid," he cried, as he hugged me with the toy between us.

John walked over, joined the hug, and moistened the last of the dry eyes in the group. "This may be the best déjà vu of my life," he said, as he quirked his head at the strange words coming out of his mouth.

"Does this seem familiar to you, too?" John asked me.

"Always!" I responded, not even sure I understood my response.

"I think we better start heading uptown before we lose the surrealness of the moment," John laughed.

"Is there such a word?" I smiled.

"Thanks to you two, there is now," he responded.

It was the heart of rush hour when we left the bookstore and boarded the D train at West 4th Street for a trip to Columbus Circle. By the time we reached our destination, the train was so packed, you could barely move. As we inched our way out of the train through an oncoming crowd that wouldn't wait for everyone to exit, Surdas lost his grip on his bag containing Biff.

"No!" he screamed, as we exited the train, and he let loose both of our hands, to retrieve his prize. Before John and I had a chance to react, the subway doors closed, and we were on the platform, watching the express train containing Surdas, who had jumped back in to rescue Biff, heading some sixty-odd blocks uptown to the next station … 125th Street.

Thirty-Two

"Bapu Gene, Bapu John, I can't find Biff," Surdas cried, not yet realizing we had been separated. "Can you help me find him? Bapu? Bapu, are you here? Bapu? Please!"

"Are you OK, son?" a strange, older, deep voice asked.

"No sir," a frightened Surdas sniffled. "I lost a gift from my parents, and when I tried to find it, I think I lost my parents. We were supposed to get off at the last stop, but I had to find my gift. It was knocked from my hand as we were trying to get through the subway doors. Can you help me find it? It's a plastic bag from the bookstore, with a stuffed bison in it. It's a gift from my dads. It means a lot to me."

"Does someone have this boy's bag?" the man demanded. "This child is blind. If someone has it, you better give the boy his damn bag, or, I swear to God, they'll be taking you out in one."

Surdas was not exactly sure how, but within a few seconds, his prize was again safely back in his hands.

"Thank you, sir," he said, as he reached to shake the older man's hand. "This is more than just a toy to me. It's kind of a treasure, because it reminds me of a character from one of my father's stories that truly moved me."

"What do you think your next move should be, young man?" the older man asked, kindly. "How do we get you back to your parents?"

"Bapu Gene, my father, said, if anything like this ever happened, I should call him, and wait at the next station."

"Good! So, you're prepared. Do you have a phone?"

"Yes sir! I have a cell phone with six express dials, one for each of my dads, one for Chris, my best friend, one for Mother, who is sort of my grandfather and foster dad at the same time, one for Dad, who is also sort of my grandfather and foster dad, and one for Uncle Josh, the rabbi."

"OK, now I'm the one who's lost," the man laughed. "That's quite a complicated family. Are you sure you're going to be all right? Do you want me to wait with you? Maybe I should wait with you."

"I'll be fine," Surdas claimed, mostly trying to assure himself. "If you'll just help make sure I get off the train with my gift, everything will be fine. I'm sure my dads will be on the next train."

When the train pulled into the125th Street station, the kindly gentleman guided Surdas to a bench, and again asked if he would like him to wait with him until his parents arrived.

"Thank you, sir, but I know my dads will be here shortly. I'll call them now, just to be safe. I will be sure to tell them of your kindness."

"You're a good boy, a brave boy," the man said, as Surdas pressed his speed dial button. "Your dads must be very proud of you. I know I am, and we just met. Take care, young man."

Thirty-Three

J ohn and I were panicked at the Columbus Circle station. The train pulled out with Surdas on board and there was no cell phone service in the station. There was little consolation in knowing that Surdas was smart enough to wait at the next station. He was a blind boy left alone in one of New York City's largest and busiest subway stations.

We must have waited a good fifteen or twenty minutes for the next train to arrive, listening to countless "We are experiencing a slight delay" and "Your train will arrive shortly" announcements during the ordeal. When the train finally did arrive, we squeezed into a car with no room to squeeze into. No one listened to our apologies and excuses. And no one complained. To everyone else, it was business as usual.

John and I were still panicked, but we were on the way … or at least we thought we were. The train moved quickly for all of two minutes, and then it suddenly stopped. It would be at least another fifteen minutes before a horrifying announcement was made. "There is police activity at 125th Street. We are sorry for the delay. Your train will be moving shortly."

Thirty-Four

Surdas was unable to reach John or me by phone, so he tried Chris. The call somehow went through, and Chris got the gist of where Surdas was, and what was happening. Before they were cut off, Chris promised to see what he could do about contacting John and me, since everyone else was hours away.

Surdas just sat there, for what seemed like hours, clutching Biff, and trying to speed dial everyone on his phone. No luck after the brief call to Chris. *At least someone knows where I am*, he thought. *Don't panic, don't cry, it's just a matter of time.*

Time can be a killer. And strange thoughts creep into your consciousness when the killer is on the loose, especially when you're a child. Surdas was deep in the middle of such thoughts, when strange hands caught hold of him, and a strange voice said, "Thank God! There you are, Buddy! Come on! Let's get out of here."

Surdas heard a loud frightened scream. He didn't even

realize at first that it was coming from him. "No, please!" he cried. "Bapu, someone … Help me … Please!"

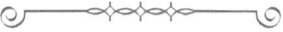

Thirty-Five

S urdas had been missing for nearly an hour by the time the police action cleared up, and our train arrived at 125th street. There was no sign of Surdas when we got off the train, but there was still a policeman on the platform.

"Excuse me," I cried, unable to contain the tears rolling down my cheeks. "Have you seen a blind boy on the platform?"

"Are either of you guys Baboon?" he asked.

"What?" we both said.

"Never mind," he responded. "Follow me. You're looking for a little blind Indian boy, right?"

"Yes! Is he OK?" I shouted. "What's going on? Where is he?"

"He's OK. There was some sort of misunderstanding. He was pretty scared and confused, so he's sitting outside the gate with his friends, sipping a milkshake, and trying to relax."

"What friends?" I said. "I don't understand."

"Welcome to the club, Buddy," he said, and then pointing outside the gate, "There he is now. And tell him I hope he finds his baboons."

And sure enough, sitting there outside the gate, between Randy and some older black gentleman that we didn't know, was Surdas, smiling and sipping on a milkshake.

"Surdas, Buddy, we're here!" John and I cried in unison.

"Where were you guys?" he cried, as he jumped up to hug us. "I must have been waiting for hours."

"We were on the next train, Buddy, but it was delayed," John said, as we continued to hug the boy. "They said there was trouble in the station, some sort of police action. What happened?"

"I got scared, because I didn't know who Randy was, and I didn't know that Sam was still here."

"What?" we both said.

"It was mostly my fault," Randy said, trying to clear things up. When Surdas couldn't reach you guys, he called Chris, who also couldn't reach you. Chris then called Chip, who then called me, because I live only a few blocks from here. I ran to the train station as quick as I could, and when I saw Surdas, I was so relieved to find the boy, that I grabbed him and told him to come with me. I was so worried for him, that I forgot he was blind, and didn't know me from Adam. He panicked, and yelled for help. And then this gentleman, who apparently helped him before, came to his rescue again."

"Sam, Sam Scott," Sam interrupted, while shaking our

hands. "I helped the boy find his gift and get off the train. He was pretty convincing that he didn't need any more help after that, but I heard there was a delay, and some problems on another platform, so I decided to wait off to the side, to make sure the boy was safe. When this young man, Randy, arrived, and the boy screamed, I rushed to help. Our encounter drew the attention of one of the policemen before everything was straightened out. But *our* misunderstanding was not the police action. We were more of a by-product."

"And then Randy bought us milkshakes to help us all calm down," Surdas chimed in.

"It was the closest thing to valium I could find on short notice," Randy laughed.

"Randy, Sam, I don't know how we could possibly thank you guys enough," John said, with tears in his eyes. "You can't imagine what we've been going through … how terrified we were."

I also wanted to thank them, but my "thank you" got caught in my throat, and I lost it … and I don't mean the "thank you." As the tears flowed, and my body began to shake, I hugged the older gentleman who had rescued my want-to-be son and his toy bison, and promised him a free copy of everything I ever wrote, and will ever write. We exchanged information, and after a round of goodbye hugs, Sam disappeared.

I then turned to Randy, hugged him as warmly as possible, and told him how wonderful a hero he was for rushing to our rescue. I told him how lucky we all are, particularly my brother Chip, to have him in our lives. I invited him to join us for the rest of the day, our treat of course, and asked him if there was any other possible way we could ever thank him.

"Don't worry," Surdas smiled. "Uncle Chip is going to take care of that. He's going to thank him in a way that has Randy shredding bedcovers."

"What?" the three of us rang out at the same time.

"When Randy called Uncle Chip to tell him that he found me, Uncle Chip said, 'I am going to thank you in such a way, that you'll be shredding all my bed covers.' Right, Randy?"

"How did you know that?" Randy said, with his mouth agape.

"I'm blind, not deaf," Surdas smiled. "My hearing is probably better than most people's. You learn to listen well when you can't see. Phone conversations from a short distance away aren't really that difficult. Want me to tell you what else he said?"

"No! Please!" Randy blushed. "Chip is so going to get it for this."

"I know," Surdas laughed. "I told you I could hear everything."

"OK, Buddy," John said coming to Randy's rescue. "We're thanking Randy for all that he's done, not torturing him. And don't even begin to go there with whatever else you heard."

"I'm sorry, Randy!" Surdas responded, sincerely. "I was just trying to be funny. I didn't mean to embarrass you."

"That's OK!" Randy said, giving Surdas a hug. "I'll know to be more careful from now on."

"Are you guys mad at me for going back to get Biff?" Surdas asked John and me sincerely. "I didn't mean to cause any problems. He means so much to me."

"Let's just say that I'm never letting you out of my sight again," I said, seriously.

"Promise?" he asked, excitedly.

And then, remembering that I was actually speaking to my parents' foster son, my foster brother, not my son, I responded, "As much as I possibly can, Buddy, as much as I possibly can."

"I'll take that as a 'Yes!' from both of you," Surdas gleamed. "Right, Biff?" he asked, as he nodded the toy in the affirmative.

The rest of our trip was as beautifully quiet and uneventful, as a trip to the most exciting city in the world can be. On Saturday afternoon, John and I stepped onto the train for the trip home, with our imaginary son in tow, only to hand my foster brother back over to my parents at journey's end. So little had changed on the outside, so much on the inside, since we left. Surdas lived in the room just across the hall from us, yet in our hearts, he was still so far away.

As for Randy, let's just say that he and Chip really did go shopping for new sheets that weekend. I have a feeling thread count wasn't a priority with these two.

Thank you, Sam, and thank you, Randy!

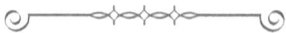

Thirty-Six

Surdas often joked that he and Hopi were the "things that go bump in the night." They weren't the only things, and the ones that followed weren't as amusing as Surdas's musings.

Robbie's career and the twins' volunteer coaching positions hit a speed bump shortly before Election Day, when the mayor and the town's two most prominent council members announced severe budget cuts for all extracurricular activities, including funding for the community college's champion football team, which Robbie coached.

The college cutbacks would make the football team's travel to play all but a few nearby teams virtually impossible, and would definitely leave the team understaffed and underequipped. Similar problems would be faced by the college's baseball, softball, basketball and soccer teams, of course, but not to the extent of the football team. They all had sponsors with deeper pockets than Robbie's fledgling team, which rarely won a game before Robbie brought them to a division championship.

The same travel predicament held true for Chip's high school soccer team, which he and Dale coached as volunteers, and on which Chris was a star player.

The school didn't even have a team a year ago. Despite very little funding from the school, and no major sponsorship, Chip and his volunteer assistant coach, Dale, had them playing, and playing well. They were the only undefeated team in the league, though they were still a point behind a team with a loss but more wins than ties. They had a great shot at the championship with only a few away games left because they were scheduled to finish the season at home against the first-place team.

Of course, that great shot depended on being able to win, and not forfeiting the few away games on their schedule before that final match.

The budget cuts would have been difficult enough for the brothers to take, but what made them particularly irksome, was that at the same time the mayor and council were announcing budget cuts, they were instituting previously approved increases in their salaries. Despite numerous protests to the school board and the college's board of directors, Robbie and Chip were told there was really not much either board could do. With the mayor and two of the four council members supporting the cuts and pay increases, passage was virtually assured.

Historically, neither the mayor nor his two cronies ever lost an election. They never even came close to losing because no one ever bothered to run against them. And because they appeared so powerful, there was very little impetus in the community to buck anything they did. Although an election was only weeks away, once again no one bothered to run against them. One way or a Mother, that was about to change.

At Mother's urging, Robbie and Chip started a petition to get the mayor and council to change their minds about the budget cuts and explore other alternatives to meet their budget requirements … like forfeiting their salary increases. They rallied all the students in the various schools to collect signatures from family members, neighbors, establishment owners, mailmen, policemen, firemen, and anyone else they could think of who lived in town. Within a week, they collected signatures from over 65% of a population that systematically had never bucked the system.

The mayor addressed the petition and the signers' concerns by saying it was simply a matter of economics, and that maybe the schools, the students, and the parents should be the ones exploring other alternatives, like bake sales, and fundraisers … maybe even some sort of show.

That was a mistake. This was not a group that you suggest a show to. The mayor and his allies were about to get their share of Show and Tell.

The family all met in Mother and Dad's house to discuss various options and plans. They were trying to come up with some sort of attention grabber to get the media behind their petition effort, when Surdas mentioned that he had heard of a similar problem in a public broadcasting program. The program focused on a young man who, trying to get a safety ordinance passed in some midwestern town, ran against an unbeatable politician, and, by doing so, gained enough publicity to get the ordinance approved. Surdas suggested that if Robbie ran against the mayor, and Chip and I ran against the other two council members supporting him, we could probably generate that type of publicity.

"Just think of all the publicity traps they could fall into," Mother agreed excitedly. "They could claim you're a family trying to take over the town. That's a headline. Or worse for them, they could claim you're trying to turn the town into some sort of gay Mecca. The media would certainly be all over that.

"Even if the mayor and councilmen try to ignore you, it would be hard for the media to ignore three gay brothers, running at the same time, in the same town, especially since you're the ones running to protect the interests of the children."

"It actually sounds like a pretty plausible idea," Robbie agreed. "But the problem is, we all have careers and family interests, and don't have time to run campaigns, especially in such a short amount of time."

"And you shouldn't," Surdas smiled. "It's not like you want to win. You just want the publicity behind your ideas. Let the other family members, who are retired, and the students and parents who are affected by the budget cuts, help.

"You could set up one campaign headquarters for all three of you, where everyone can volunteer. Your parents and Uncle Josh could run the campaign. And if you really want to gain publicity, put Auntie Sue and Auntie Allie in charge of promotion."

"I'm not exactly sure how you mean that, Sweetie," Aunt Sue responded, "but I must say that I'm rather intrigued by the idea. If anyone knows about camp pains, it's Allie and me."

Surdas laughed, "The sky's the limit, so why not start with the stars."

"There is no small sin in a lack of sincerity," Aunt Sue chuckled. "Still, your flattery never ceases to be sin-sational. I'm in … and so is Allie."

"So is Allie what?" Aunt Allie asked, clueless.

"I can't even imagine how many people have asked that question," Aunt Sue responded. "In! In with the whole idea."

"Oh, good! I hate being out."

"Don't give me lines like that, girlfriend," Aunt Sue chuckled. "You were in, with out, way before out was ever in. Everybody knows, that when you were born, they didn't even bother to cut the boa."

Thirty-Seven

Much to our chagrin, little attention was paid to the announcements that Robbie was going to run against the incumbent mayor, Chip was going to run against the town council member from town center, and I was opposing the councilman from the area where the rest of our family lived. We were actually more of a toe-note, than a footnote, in the local newspaper.

To make matters worse, it was also much more difficult to obtain the required signatures to get us on the ballot, than it was to collect them to oppose the budget cuts. Apparently, people in small towns do not like to buck incumbents, especially when there are so many ways that their bucks are incumbent upon them.

After a few days of little success in collecting signatures, the family met once again to discuss strategy. The aunts were noticeably missing from the meeting, which seemed to be going nowhere. The meeting had just about come to an unsuccessful conclusion, when suddenly the door burst open, and the aunts entered in their finest feathered regalia, singing "There's No Business Like Show Business."

As the aunts paraded around the room, lifting the spirits of all its occupants, Chris whispered a description of the entire amazing spectacle in Surdas's ear. His smile and giggle lit up the room as much as the aunts did.

"Thanks!" Robbie chuckled, as the aunts finished their number. "We all needed a lift."

"Oh! This is more than a lift, Baby," Aunt Sue smiled. "This is a high-heeled elevation of your election strategy. This is liftoff, as we turn to the stars. We've rented out the entire movie theater for this Wednesday, and we are going to put on a free show … a show this town will never forget.

"You're looking at the wake-up call for this little town that always sleeps. Their alarm is about to become alarming. And there will be more surprises than just the first drag show to hit the yokel theater. All you boys will need to do, is hang out at the back of the theater to answer any questions at the end. There will be students there collecting signatures to get you three on the ballot. Even if you don't get enough people to sign, we should at least gain enough publicity to get your funding issue in the press."

"It truly sounds wonderful," I added, "but how do we get people, who are worried about signing, to come to the event."

"We don't play it up as a signature drive. We play it up as a free need-for-funding awareness show, entitled *Funding Is a Drag*. We won't even mention the signature tables at the end of the show. The guests will realize they're there at the end. Right now, all they need to know is the magic word … free.

"What do ya think?"

Mother stood up, walked over to Aunt Sue and Aunt Allie, and in his best Ethel Merman voice sang, "Yesterday they told you you would not go far … Let's go on with the show."

"What do you think?" Chris whispered to Surdas.

"I think this is the best family ever," he chuckled.

Thirty-Eight

Mother and the aunts wasted no time in putting a show together that revolved around kids, education, and the importance of extracurricular activities. Robbie, Chip, and Dale spearheaded a drive to have the students in all the schools, and the community college, invite their parents to attend the show. Mark, John, and I worked on publicity, including posters and fliers. And Uncles Josh and Mohammed helped Dad spread them all over town.

On the night of the show, to our surprise, the theater was not only packed, it was standing room only.

Aunt Allie led off with a parody of his Marlene Dietrich specialty, titled "Failing at Sports Again." Aunt Sue followed with a rousing Rihanna impersonation of "Don't Stop the Music." Mother took the tag with an Ethel Merman parody: "I've No Rhythm, I've No Music." The three divas then performed hilarious versions of "Beauty School Dropout," "Charlie Brown," "School Daze (Days)," "Teach

Your Children," and finished with the Nat King Cole standard "You Don't learn That in School," and Bob Dylan's "Forever Young."

As our three stars left the stage to a rousing standing ovation, it began to fill with children, ranging from grade school to college students. Almost all of them had parents in the audience. As Chris led the last child, Surdas, to the center of the stage, the students broke out into a spectacular version of the Beach Boys' classic, "Be True to Your School." Then, as they finished, Surdas bravely took a few steps forward.

"My name is Surdas Patel," he began. "I am blind. Hopefully, you are not. Your children, your future, the people who need and trust in you most, are up here asking for your help. The activities that we have come to love, and that you have guided us through, are being taken away from us while the monies that could save them are being poured into pockets that can afford to remain closed. We are powerless to change this. You are not. You can save our games, our music, our arts, our clubs, our times of doing something progressive together, and molding our character, and perhaps our future.

"There are people in the back of the room who care about us, the way we hope you do too. They are running for office, spending their valuable time to save the programs we rely on. All of us up here are asking you to sign their petitions to get them on the ballot. Not just for them, for us. That's why they're doing it. That's why we're doing it. Hopefully, that's why you'll be doing it too.

"If you feel like you've been blindsided by this part of the show, you're right. It was my idea, and, as I have told you, I am blind. But I am not too blind to see that it was necessary to open your eyes. Our wonderful performers and our superb candidates for office did not know that we were hijacking the end of the show. This is your family, your village telling you that we need you. And …"

> If we shadows have offended,
> Think but this, and all is mended,
> That you have but slumber'd here
> While these visions did appear.
> And this weak and idle theme,
> No more yielding but a dream,
> Gentles, do not reprehend:
> If you pardon, we will mend.
> Give us your hands, if we be friends,
> (Shakespeare)

And use your signature to make amends.

Good night!"

"And please remember, that 'the play's the thing,' which will also be cut."

Drag stars, children singing, Shakespeare, a little blind wizard … there was magic in the air, and magic on paper. Robbie, Chip, and I had enough signatures on our petitions to file our candidacies the next morning. Not only did we make the front page of the local paper, but a video of the show also went viral on the internet, and by evening, we were national news.

"Gay Brothers Protect Town's Children Against the Cutting Agenda of Local Politicians," read one headline. "Local Family *Drags* Elected Officials Through the Mud They Created," read another. Thanks to the aunts' and Surdas's spin, the world was turning upside down.

Thirty-Nine

Suction sucks! And the tentacles of political power have plenty of suction. A few days after the *Funding Is a Drag* show, a registered letter from the Board of Directors of the children's home arrived, informing Mother and Dad that a mistake had apparently been made in the processing of their foster care application for Surdas, as both foster parents were older than the criteria established in the facility's guidelines.

Moreover, the letter stated, the children's home was currently exploring a more suitable environment for Surdas, "given the gravity of his special needs." Gravity also sucks, by the way … especially when the gravity is bureaucratic.

A quick phone call from Mother and Dad to the children's home revealed that the director, whom they had dealt with in the past, was on "an unplanned leave." The new acting director would only tell them that the age restriction policy had always been in effect for the protection of the children, and that somehow Mother and Dad's ages had been overlooked in the processing of their application. He apologized for the unfortunate mistake, and informed them that the facility was currently preparing for Surdas's return and proper placement.

The bomb was a Mother lode that could be heard throughout the entire property.

Forty

Surdas and I were working on a writing exercise in my room, when Mother exploded, and frantically burst through the door, seeking advice on how best to handle the situation with the children's home. His effort to find the best way to handle the situation, probably would have been handled much better, if he had noticed Surdas was in the room with me, when he expletively blurted out the news. In the heat of the moment, he forgot that this was one of those times Surdas would probably be there. I think Mother just wanted to lie down and die, when Surdas gasped, "Oh, No! Please don't let them take me away," from an obstructed corner of the room.

"Don't worry, Baby," Mother cried, as he ran over and hugged Surdas. "We'll figure something out. Where there's a will, there's a way. And anyone who tries to take you away, better have a will, a last one, because I will certainly put them away, and out of my misery."

"Calm down, guys," I implored them both. "Let me

talk to John. This is kind of sudden, but I'm pretty sure we may be able to come up with a plausible solution."

"Solution? What solution?" Mother asked, frenzied, just as John walked through the door. "If you have a solution, pour it on the table."

"Your Dad told me what happened," John said, as he came over and kissed me. "What do you think, Babe?"

"I don't even have to," I smiled.

"Then we're ready?" he asked, knowingly.

"What do *you* think?"

"You know I don't have to either!" he responded, joyfully.

"OK then!"

"OK then what?" Mother gasped. "Who am I, Alan Turing? You're both going to be speaking in remorse code if you don't decipher your little cipher and tell me what the hell is going on."

"OK! How would you like another grandchild?" I asked.

"Please just tell me what you're talking about, Genie. I'm too riddled in frantic for you to riddle me anything else."

"John and I have grown very fond of Surdas. It's no big secret. And, for a while, we've been thinking about adding to our family. It's even one of the reasons that we moved here. If Surdas will have us, and if you and Dad are comfortable with a little switch in family dynamics that will keep Surdas with us, we just may have an adaptable, adoptable solution.

"If *we* adopt Surdas, it really wouldn't change things

too much, as far as you and Dad are concerned. It's not like any of us are very good at taking care of ourselves. You'd be needed as much as ever.

"You have been doing a great job with Surdas's care and education. It would be a great disservice to him, if you guys and Uncle Josh didn't continue. Even when our house is completed, we'll be only a few yards away. We can still eat all our meals here and help with chores after our place is finished, if you'll have us. So, things won't be very different than they are now. And John and I can even help with the food bill, after I win my first Pulitzer, or Surdas wins his."

"Why does sounding like I'm getting the worst of the deal, make me so happy?" Mother laughed.

"It's a Mother thing," I smiled. "Only you would understand."

Mother yelled down to Dad, "Tom, come up here and give your sons and grandchild a hug," and then walked over and kissed John and me.

"Thank you, boys, for keeping our family together," he said, lovingly. "I'm so proud of both of you. And I'm so happy for all of us. I know we can make this work. Anyway, Dad and I will be much better at grandparenting than parenting. It will make it that much easier to spoil Surdas rotten."

"You don't need to thank us," John responded. "Just like you and Dad, we truly love Surdas. It's an act of love all the way around. But I think we better find out what our prospective son has to say, before we get too excited about making any new parenting arrangements."

"So, what do you think, Buddy?" I asked Surdas, who was still sitting in the corner, only now with this happy dumbfounded grin on his face. "Will you have a fledgling writer and a newbie minister to be your lawfully recognized parents?"

"Surely my magical family already knows the answer," Surdas smiled, as tears flowed down his cheeks. "I have found a home in a family of genies, who know how to make all my wishes come true. This is my fondest wish of all, the greatest honor anyone can ever give me. What better solution, when only the titles switch around, not the love. And the whole getting spoiled rotten deal doesn't sound too rotten to me either. Although, I can't imagine how Mother and Dad are going to improve on perfection."

"That's the first time you called us by our family names," Mother said, somewhat surprised.

"That's because I finally understand that I am part of this magical family," he replied.

Surdas then made his way over to John and me and took our hands. "In India, they use the term 'Bapu,' to denote respect for one's father. I dreamed, but never really thought, that I would have the opportunity to call you so. But Bapu Gene and Bapu John, you must also know that you have always had more than just my respect. Truly, you have always had my love. I would be most honored to be your beta, or son."

As I hugged my prospective beta, I recalled him whispering the word "Bapu" on more than a few occasions. Was this something he somehow always knew?

Once again, before the opportunity of raising the question even had an opportunity to cross my mind, Surdas changed the subject, and brought an air of comic relief to the room, by seriously turning toward Mother, and adding, "And perhaps, Dear Uncle, as I have been so honored, may I now be so privileged to call you not Mother, but Grandmother."

"It beats Madeleine's calling me Mothra," Mother laughed as he gave Surdas a huge hug, "but I think I still prefer being called Mother. It has a little more of a youthful and familiar ring to it. And it will prevent me from slapping you in the back of your head, if you even think of addressing me as grandmother in public."

"Mother it is," Surdas laughed.

Just then Dad walked through the door. "What's all the fuss about up here?" he asked, rather knowingly.

"It took you so long to get up here," Mother teased, "we had a ten-year-old grandson in between, Grandpa."

"Maybe that's why I took so long," Dad smiled. "I've been looking forward to another grandson. Are we spoiling him yet?"

Forty-One

The next morning, Mother and Dad accompanied John and me to the children's home to clear up all the confusion, and file adoption papers for Surdas.

We were sitting in the office of one of the counselors, discussing the adoption papers, when the new acting director barged in and interrupted, "Don't get your hopes up, nor the boy's. The institute has been exploring a more appropriate situation for Surdas's special needs, and would, of course, come to a decision that is in the best interests of the boy."

"But the boy loves his family—this family," Mother protested. "That makes staying with this family his best interests."

"I understand your sentiment," the acting director said, almost flippantly. "We will take everything in the boy's interests into consideration. You can rest assured, he will be placed in a family appropriate to those interests."

"That's absurd! The family who loves him, and who he

loves, is the family most appropriate to those interests," I protested. "There is no way in hell that we are going to lose him. If you even think of exploring other options, you will have a lawsuit and media debacle, unlike anything you have ever seen before."

"Think about it," he started to say. "Do you really want to drag the boy through that and sue —"

Before he even finished the sentence, the office door swung open, and in walked Aunt Sue.

"Call my name, call my name ... yes, they do! They definitely want Sue. And here I am!

"Excuse me for not interrupting earlier," Aunt Sue snickered at the acting director, as he marched mere inches away from his face, "but I was having such a good time listening to you build a verbal guillotine for you and your family, that I couldn't pry my ear away from the door, until your crooked little neck was firmly in place."

And then, turning toward the rest of us who were sitting there quite astounded, he continued, "Before our young acting director here squeezes his fat head further through the guillotine hole he just bored for himself, let me just tell you, that in two weeks, Gene and Surdas will join Robbie and Chip on stage for a very special Ellen show. It's amazing the reach a viral video like our little show had.

"Ellen wants to discuss the election and Surdas's moving performance on behalf of the children of the town. I expect that the intended adoption of Surdas by Gene and John will also be one of the main topics of conversation.

"Of course, if there were to be any complications with

the adoption, the conversation may lean more toward the extremely unqualified acting, and I use that term, 'acting,' as loosely as possible, director who is trying to remove the poor boy from his loving family. You know, the acting director who was recently appointed by his father, the chairman of the home's Board of Directors, who, quite coincidentally, is married to the sister of the sitting mayor, whom Robbie is running against.

"Not quite the feel-good story of the adoption that Ellen might prefer, but a hell of a lot more newsworthy, wouldn't you say?

"That kind of story could come back to bite the mayor in the ass, providing he could tear the lips of his nephew here away from it."

The all-knowing smile left Aunt Sue's face, as he seriously returned his gaze toward the acting director. "My suggestion, Mr. Acting Director, is that you wipe that shitty little cheesy grin off your little rat face, crawl back into whatever hole your daddy dragged you out of, and call him. Tell him that the plan sucks as much as his family does, and, whatever it takes, the two of you better get the adoption paperwork signed, sealed and delivered, before the show in two weeks. If this story leaks, and I'm quite sure it could, it will run all the way down to your family's sewer."

"But that's—" the director started to say.

"Enough!" Aunt Sue said, snapping his fingers. "That's more than enough. You have precious little time to straighten out this crooked little game of yours, Mr. Acting Director. So, you had better quit acting, and get your act together. We're playing for real now. You'd better hurry up and get that way."

The acting director stood there frozen for a minute or two, as though he were melting in Aunt Sue's gaze. As he visibly tried to piece together all that just broke in front of him, he turned to leave without saying a word.

"I hope my cross words are not a puzzle to you, little man," Aunt Sue sneered at the acting director's retreat, "because your grieving relatives will find the solution to the puzzle, buried at 6 down and 5 across, if you ever mess with my family again.

"Oh! One more thing for you to think about before you leave. This family represents all that is good. Your family represents all that is evil. When it comes to the battle of good against evil, whatever side I'm on, is going to win. Remember that! And remember it well! Because when it comes to being evil, I'm damn good."

Mother, Dad, John, and I sat there with our mouths agape through the whole scenario. It must have taken us quite a few minutes after the acting director left to finally comprehend what had just happened, and regain the power of speech.

"Is all of this true?" I finally asked, not even sure what part of the story my mind was focusing on.

"Of course, Baby, all of it. I don't come to shootouts bluffing. I come packing ... and I don't take survivors."

"But how did you know and do all this?"

"It's star power, Baby, simple cosmology. Anything can

happen when the star aligns. I'm a star, so that's what I did. I aligned myself, and used my grave-intentional pull.

"I told you, Sweetie, I led lives that have lives of their own, and met plenty of other lives along the way. I know people who know people, that nobody else knows. Everybody has a few loose strings. I know how to pull them.

"As for Ellen, she and I go way back. We have a few secrets of our own. I left the information for the show on everyone's bed. Make sure that you're there early. Allie and I will be in the green room for makeup duty."

And before we could even thank him, Aunt Sue slipped out the door and disappeared, but not before we heard the acting director yell "Ow!" from down the hall.

Forty-Two

While all this was going on, a nervous Surdas was at home with Uncle Josh, working on one of their many homeschool lessons. After the lesson, Surdas surprised Uncle Josh by asking, "Do you think that people are randomly born with disabilities, or is there some sort of higher power that, for one reason or another, thrust the situation upon them."

"A wise man might try to answer your question, My Son," Uncle Josh smiled sadly, "but a wiser one would not. You are asking a dot to explain the mind that created everything in the universe and more. I would be quite a foolish dot to think that I understand the thoughts and workings of the Creator of all things known and unknown. No part truly comprehends the whole, and certainly not such a tiny part. The fact that we are discovering new things every day, is proof of it. There is more to God than meets the 'I,' meaning, in this case, the pronoun. I believe to believe anything else, is to create God in Man's own image, instead of the other way around.

"There are billions of people on this planet alone. There may be billions of other planets, each with billions more beings inhabiting them. Everything in creation appears to have its own special purpose, its own special needs, and its own special handicaps.

"Does the Creator truly play such an important role in the development of each and every one of his creations, that He takes the time to design and attend to every minute detail? Are there evolutionary processes at work that might escape His handiwork? Do we, His creations, have a choice, and choose the path ourselves before we even get here? Is it fate? Karma? A roll of the dice? Does anyone, outside of the Creator, truly have a clue? I think not.

"I often think, none of it is truly significant enough in the Creator's scheme of things, that He pays strict attention to it all. He may have no limits, but I can't imagine that He doesn't allow Himself a few limitations.

"The Tao Te Ching, a classic text that we should read someday, says, 'The Tao does nothing, yet leaves nothing undone.' By that, of course, it is referring to the Creator. It is a quote that I find hard to disagree with. But then again, who can possibly disagree with anything that they can't possibly fully understand?

"As you can probably guess, I don't pretend to have a clue, as to how to truly answer your question. So, let me address it in a different way.

"My father, who was also a rabbi, used to say, 'Life is

like a huge deck of cards.' Not the most spiritual of sayings, but then again, my father was not the most spiritual of men. However, he knew how to make a point. I say this knowing that every time you judge another's spirituality, you diminish your own.

"My father believed everyone is dealt a hand. Some hands appear to be far more advantageous than others, but everyone still gets to choose from the deck. Every person's success or failure depends on how they play their hand … what they hold onto, what they dispose of, and how much they're willing to draw.

"A stacked hand misplayed, is of far less value, than a supposed weak hand well played. The real winners are the ones who play the best hands they can, no matter what the circumstances, because the circumstances are only in effect for the duration of the game.

"The good news is there are no losers. In the end, everyone gets to share in the pot anyway. The only bad news is, that you may have to keep playing until you play your hand correctly. The game eventually ends, but the pot goes on forever.

"His point was, there are advantages and disadvantages to every hand that is dealt in life. In the end, no matter how much we bluff, no matter how high we raise the ante, it's only the way we play the hand that counts. All the chips belong to the Creator anyway. In the end, He's the One who is going to gather them in. So why not play the game the way it appears He wants us to play … His way."

Uncle Josh gently rubbed his hand through Surdas's

hair. "I'm afraid that my answer did more to question your question than answer it, My Boy. If I've left you with even more questions and things to think about than before, perhaps I have, in some way, succeeded. Perhaps the question is the answer in itself, the same way that the Creator is ultimately the answer to every question about Him."

Surdas thanked Uncle Josh, and walked away feeling that he more or less knew more and less than he did before. He was just glad that Chris wasn't there. He thought Chris's head would have truly exploded.

Forty-Three

The next Friday, less than a week before the Ellen show, Surdas's adoption papers arrived. He was ecstatic. He had a new family, and the chance to dance with Ellen, all in the same week.

"This is the best day of my life," he exclaimed, as we read the adoption papers to him.

"You say that every day," Chris replied, teasingly.

"You say that, like it's a bad thing," Surdas responded. "Seems to me, it's a pretty good way to live your life … and an even better reason to look forward to tomorrow."

"You're a pretty smart kid," Chris admitted, smiling at the simplicity of the logic.

"I picked you for a best friend, didn't I?" Surdas smiled.

"OK! You're a very smart kid. Are you nervous about the show?"

"I'd feel better if you were there with me."

"You'll be fine. You'll be there with your dad, my dad,

and Chip. And I'll be there. I'll just be in the audience with our other dads and the rest of the family."

"I know, but I see everything so much better when you're whispering it to me. You know how to help me see everything better than anyone. I miss so much when you're not there."

"I'll tell you what," Chris assured him. "We'll record the show, and that night, we'll have a sleepover, and I'll whisper to you everything that went on as though it was happening right then. What do you think?"

"I think that will be the best day of my life," Surdas laughed.

Forty-Four

The following week, Molly and Lauren agreed to babysit Madeleine, so that the rest of the family could join Robbie, Chip, Surdas, and me for the taping of the Ellen show. When we arrived, the four of us who were to be on the show were taken immediately for makeup and instructions, sans the disappointed aunts, and then to the Green Room. The rest of the family, including the disappointed makeup-laden aunts, were taken to prime seats in the audience.

A short while before the taping was to begin, Ellen stopped in to personally welcome us, and make sure that we were comfortable. When she introduced herself to Surdas, and gave him a hug, I was sure he was going to faint from the excitement. He opened his mouth to say something to her, and for the first time since I laid eyes on him, the words wouldn't come out.

"Are you nervous?" Ellen asked.

Surdas nodded his head.

"Is there anything I can do?" she asked, sympathetically.

Surdas nodded his head again.

"Can you tell me what it is without nodding?" she laughed.

"Chris," he blurted out.

"Who's Chris?"

Suddenly, at the thought of his best friend and hero, Surdas regained his voice, and everything that was locked inside him poured out.

"Chris is kind of like my soul brother, though he's really more like my adopted cousin. He's my best friend, and my eyes whenever I need them, which is most of the time.

"He tells me everything that's going on better than anyone can. So it's like I can really see it, even though I can't. He even saved my life a few times, although he's the one that put it in danger each time, only maybe not really. Still, he's a real hero, and the reason I'm here today, in more ways than one … literally."

"Wow! Chris is quite a mouthful," Ellen smiled. "Anything else?"

"Even though my father and uncles are with me," Surdas responded shyly, "and I love them, and they make me feel safe and at ease, it would be so much better if Chris were with me too."

"So Chris would kind of be like icing on the cake?" Ellen laughed.

"Oh, no!" Surdas exclaimed. "To me he's more like the cake, and everything else is the icing."

"Well, we can't have just icing, can we?" she asked. "Is he here now?"

"He's in the audience with the rest of the family, and he'll probably want to kill me for asking for him, because he's kind of shy, but it would be so worth it. And he'd probably just save my life again, anyway."

"OK then! Let's get Chris in here," she laughed. "Is there anything else?"

"Is he going to dance with us?" Surdas asked, sincerely.

"Are we dancing together?" Ellen asked, quite surprised.

"Well, Mother, who's actually my grandfather, and Aunt Sue, who's actually my great-auntie or uncle, it gets confusing sometimes, have been teaching me to dance like you all week. Mother said it would be a once in a lifetime opportunity, that I shouldn't deprive either of us of, if the opportunity arose."

"Mother sounds very wise," Ellen responded, trying to sound serious.

"So he tells me," Surdas replied, dutifully.

"Well then," Ellen said, "it looks like Chris is going to be dancing with us."

"Cool!" Surdas smiled, excitedly. "Let's not tell him till it's time. Everyone says he dances like a turkey. I don't want him to chicken out. I bet that's one description he won't be whispering in my ear when he sees the video."

"You gotta love this kid," Ellen laughed, looking at the three adults in the room.

"You're preaching to the choir," I smiled. "He has a magic and a majesty that's all his own."

"Well, Your Majesty," Ellen said, as she knelt down and straightened Surdas's tie, "is there anything else?"

"How about a lucky kiss for a really good show?" he smiled.

"Sure!" she said, as she kissed his cheek. "But I really don't think you'll need it."

"Oh! I didn't mean for me," he laughed, with a wink in his smile.

Forty-Five

Later that night, Chris and Surdas had their sleepover as promised. Surdas was ecstatic. Chris was somewhat less than so.

"Oh, come on, Chris," Surdas entreated. "We had a great time. You have to admit that it was kind of magical. And our entrance wasn't really that bad."

"That's easy for you to say, Dancing Boy. You weren't the one that tripped Ellen into the audience, doing that stupid dance."

"It wasn't stupid. It was fun. And they said they would cut out the part where you both landed in the lap of that heavy lady who couldn't stop laughing."

"Yeah, but somehow I know that it is going to wind up on *YouTube* or some blooper show."

"That would be so cool! I can see it now," Surdas giggled.

"You know, you are so freaky, sometimes you scare me," Chris caught himself smiling. "Do you ever take anything seriously?"

"Sure, just not things involving you. Seriously, you're too serious."

"I'm too serious? Who's the one who everyone thinks is a five-hundred-year-old saint. I'm the one who's been teaching you how to be a kid, remember?"

"See, my plan is working. You have to constantly act like some happy-go-lucky kid, in order for me to feel like one. My job to lighten you up, is right on target. I am the sun to your moon."

"Great! You're a star, and I'm some sort of revolving space ball."

"I'd say that's probably what Ellen is thinking right now," Surdas laughed.

"You are so getting tickled into a pee puddle, Sunny Boy," Chris promised, as he launched his attack.

"Bring it on, Space Ball," Surdas laughed, unable to contain his delight.

This time, no amount of begging or threatening would help. Surrender was not an option, except for Surdas's bladder.

Forty-Six

The Ellen interview was a big boost for all our campaigns. Surdas's interview went splendidly, and Chip and I let Robbie do most of the adult talking on the show. We all kept our focus on the importance of education and extracurricular activities for children, and never once mentioned our opponents, or their records during the taping.

The audience, which was mostly made up of women, was more than receptive to our concerns, and gave us a rousing ovation at the end. And, although I believe they were pleased with everything they heard, I am convinced that most of the ovation was for Mother and the aunts' surprise ending "Take A Chance On Me" drag number, which they performed as the "Abba Cadavers."

Much to Chris's delight, it was the ending number that went viral on the internet, not Ellen's trip into the audience. By week's end, Robbie, Chip, and I were all polling within single digits of our opponents, and the local paper was calling for debates between all the candidates. As Surdas had predicted, we were being heard. It was not surprising, therefore, that the empire, once again, struck back.

Forty-Seven

One of the best places to find small minds, is in small towns, where diversity is a four-letter word, which is seldom spoken in public, much less practiced in private.

No one in town paid any attention to any of the residents in our little compound, until a few days after the Ellen show. Then a group calling itself "The Moral Majority for the American Way" decided to hold a decency rally in support of the mayor and the two councilmen, to set the record "straight," as to how the town felt about being "dragged" into a state of moral decline. The group's posters, advertising the event, depicted Mother and the aunts performing in costume, while two little boys watching their show put on lipstick and eye shadow. "THE AGENDA BEHIND THE PERFORMANCE!" the caption read.

I'd say that they stirred up the Mother of all hornets' nests, if the nest of aunts wasn't so much fiercer.

On the night of the rally, Mother and the aunts each stood outside the three entrances to the hall where the rally was being held, handing out free swastikas, white KKK dunce hats, and large "I'm With Stupid" buttons, to everyone entering. It took quite a while before anyone connected with the rally realized what was happening, and the police were called to remove the dragsters from the hall's property.

Aunt Sue anticipated their removal … and was prepared. He put on a tiara and a sash that read "Miss Direction" (homonyms are a drag queen forte) and began successfully sending people to the wrong rally site. "Hurry along," he would tell them as he advised them of a change in venue. "Everybody who is nobody is going to be there. You simply must go. Time waits for no one … and that's you, Baby. Hurry along."

The amazing part was, that apparently only a few of the people attempting to attend the rally caught the sarcasm. But the press certainly did and jumped on it. The rally and comical diversion tactics actually cost the incumbents a few more percentage points from the increasingly embarrassed electorate, and all three races were now considered statistically too close to call.

The mayor and councilmen were forced to agree to debates. They each agreed to one debate the week before the election, and scheduled Chip's debate first. It was on a Thursday night, when his team was scheduled to play the championship soccer game. My debate was scheduled for the following evening, when I was supposed to do a book reading at the local library. And Robbie's debate against the mayor was scheduled the day after mine, and set for the exact time Robbie's football team was playing their biggest game of the year against their team rival.

Coincidence? … Or a stroke of scheduling genius? Since there are no coincidences, nor geniuses behind the incumbents' campaigns, your guess is as good as mine.

The schedulers apparently forgot, however, that Dale was every bit the player and coach that Chip was. So Chip confidently left the soccer game in Dale's hands on the night of the first debate. Between Dale's coaching and Chris's goaltending, their team won the championship by defeating their opponent almost as soundly as Chip defeated his. The quite unprepared, nervous, and balding older councilman was no match for the confident and strikingly handsome younger man, who spoke so eloquently, and who unselfishly gave so much of his free time to coach and mentor the youth of the town. The incumbent trio were already in check at the opening moves of their chess match.

I was able to reschedule my book reading for the next week, and was up next. On the way to Town Centre, Aunt Sue gave me the same advice he gave Chip. "If you want to make people appreciate you, always arrive late. Important people never arrive on time. Let them be thankful that you managed to squeeze them into your busy schedule. A little bit of gratitude goes a long way in making it seem like you're doing them a favor by being there, instead of the other way around. That's why drag queens invented Gay Time.

Chip's draw in the pool might have been considered a bit of a bottom-feeder, but mine was more of a shark. I wasn't intimidated, however, because the point was to get our funding point across, not necessarily to win the debate. I may have been a bit ahead on looks, but he was way ahead on experience and accomplishments. I can only assume he was also way ahead in the debate, when for some strange reason near the end, he flippantly remarked how strangely odd and unnatural it was that my mother was a man, and that we call ourselves a family, although none of us are even remotely related. This pitch was a curve I could hit.

"Actually," I replied, "I would have thought you were intelligent enough to understand that 'mother' reference to be physically impossible—unless, of course, your comment was meant to be some sort of homophobic slur, in which case you would be figuratively smarter and literally dumber than the comment.

"The person you are obviously referring to, is my uncle, who adopted me, and became one of my two fathers, soon after my mother passed away. He is referred to, by all who know him, as Mother, because of his loving and compassionate nature, and his unique ability to raise the spirit, and to nurture the soul of all those fortunate enough to make his acquaintance. It is an opportunity you should avail yourself of. I'm sure that you would greatly benefit from the experience.

"Mother, and my other father, Mother's husband, Tom, whom we all refer to as Dad, adopted me and three other lost children, took us under their wings, gave us wings of our own, and raised us to a height where three of us, with promising careers, are now running for office in this town.

"They taught us, there is no one born less noble, less worthy, or less equal, than the highest among us. They taught us, that everyone is important, that everyone should have the ability to get ahead, and that no one should be left behind. They taught us, that every life is a gift from God, and all of God's gifts are to be respected and treated as such, whether we understand them or not. And they taught us, that what you are called is far less important than what you are called upon to do, especially unto others.

"Just do it, and do it justly, we were taught. We are all opportunity knocking. Those who follow us cannot answer if there is no one, no opportunity knocking at their door.

"Cutting school programs is abandoning the door. It is closing and barring all the windows of opportunity that we have availed ourselves of in our past. We have been given so much more than those before us, because of their willingness to sacrifice. Why would we wish so much less for those that follow? Should we be any less willing to sacrifice for them?

"Our children, our future, and our legacy are waiting at the door for opportunity to knock. I plan to be there knocking so that others can answer and open the door to their future. I hope you will all join me. That's the difference between an opportunist and an opportunity. I plan to be an opportunity.

"And one more thing … you have no idea what a family means, if you think it is only formed by blood. While most of my family is unrelated by blood, they perfectly relate to each other in love. Relatively speaking, that's what makes a true family. A true family is based on love. Love is thicker than blood. It's even thicker than you."

None of what I said was planned. It was a knee-jerk response, to a knee from a jerk. I was shocked and shaken by the ovation that followed. The response had ended the debate, and apparently my opponent's advantage. Check, again!

Two down, one more debate to go.

Forty-Eight

The next morning everyone met for a buffet breakfast at Mother and Dad's home. Considering the recent turn of events, the entire family was abuzz about Robbie's chances against the mayor in the debate later that evening. Like the good quarterback that he was, Robbie seemed to be handling the pressure well. Like the good husband that he is, Mark played defense and kept the pressure from getting to his teammate.

Robbie was actually more nervous about the big game that his college football team would be playing without him, than he was about the debate. He felt that as far as the election was concerned, they had already made the point about the budget cuts, and if the mayor would only back down, he would withdraw from the race and coach his team to victory.

But despite the recent setbacks, the mayor didn't back down. Robbie was going to have to miss the game. And, since his two assistants found safer positions as soon as the budget cuts were announced, he was going to have to rely on soccer enthusiasts Chip and Dale to coach his football team to victory.

The drama and trauma of the morning's political conversations and coaching preparations were becoming too much for the younger members of the family, who, for the most part, were left out of the conversations anyway. So Chris took off to spend some quiet time with Molly. Surdas, saddened by the departure, decided to take a walk around the property with Madeleine and Hopi.

Neither Surdas nor Hopi were in the habit of traveling more than the limits of the property by themselves. But with their four-year-old guide firmly in charge, they decided to venture a bit farther. They were walking through property completely unfamiliar to them a mile or so away, when Madeleine suddenly tripped over something in the grass. She fell, scraped her knee, and began crying. Surdas stopped to assist her, and tried to bandage the scrape with a handkerchief he was carrying in his pocket. It was a difficult task, since he couldn't see the wound, and Madeleine was crying too much to be of any assistance. During the confusion, Surdas inadvertently let go of Hopi's leash.

Normally, Hopi's freedom would not have been a problem, but for some reason, as Surdas was helping the still sobbing Madeleine to her feet, Hopi inexplicably took off as if blindly chasing, or being chased by something. Surdas panicked. And with Madeleine holding his hand and guiding him, they did their best to run after Hopi.

It soon became apparent by the sound of her barking, that Hopi was traveling much faster than them, and that the wounded Madeleine couldn't keep up. Surdas, in desperation, released Madeleine's hand and ran as fast as he could in the direction of Hopi's barking. Within a few minutes, he was over a hill and out of little Madeleine's sight. She limped as quickly as she could in his direction, calling his name, but there was no response.

When she finally reached the top of the hill, Madeleine saw Hopi standing close to, what appeared to be, a steep drop on the other side. Surdas, however, was nowhere to be seen. She kept going, and when she reached the edge of the drop, she saw Surdas lying at the bottom. He wasn't moving. She called his name a few more times, the last couple while crying. He neither moved nor answered. She started screaming for help. She was in the middle of nowhere. Again, there was no answer.

Forty-Nine

Robbie was giving some last-minute coaching suggestions to Chip and Dale, when Mother's dog, Angel,
suddenly leapt to her feet, and ran to the front door, barking and scratching to get out. It was way out of character
for Mother's little helper. So we all knew that something
was wrong.

The absence of Surdas and Madeleine flashed like
a lightning bolt around the room. Dad swung the front
door open, and we all rushed after our four-legged leader,
shouting out the kids' names, while attempting to stifle the
panic. The lack of response was deafening, and we quickly
began losing sight of Angel, who was much faster than her
posse, and obviously on an urgent mission.

I was in full panic mode about losing our guide by
the time Angel completely disappeared. Then I realized
she was fully aware of our limitations, and she kept us in
the loop by continuing to bark as she ran ahead. Soon we
were able to hear Madeleine's crying in addition to An-

gel's barking. Madeleine was too upset to respond to our calls. What was most frightening, was that Surdas didn't respond either.

It is impossible to describe the extent of the fear that grabbed hold of me at the absence of my son by her side, when Madeleine came into view. Somehow, the poor child sensed the extreme dread swarming towards her, and was able to calm herself into directing us to where Surdas had fallen. Angel was already by our son's side, by the time John and I managed to slide our way down the embankment.

Surdas was unconscious, but he was breathing. I found myself thanking God for that much at least, as the dirt on his face began to turn into mud from the tears that began to rain down upon him. *I am not going to lose you,* I silently kept promising him. *I just found you. I am never going to lose you again.* I saw similar prayers in the tears in John's eyes.

Mark had already phoned for help, before John and I were conscious enough to call out for any. Then he quickly left Madeleine in the care of her grandparents, and joined Robbie, Chip, and Dale by our side at the bottom of the embankment, as we waited for an ambulance. It was an all too real surreal experience, that probably lasted only a fraction of the time it seemed.

Fifty

S urdas was still unconscious when the ambulance arrived. After a quick examination, the medics lifted Surdas onto a stretcher, placed him in the ambulance, and John and I rode along with him. The rest of the family took Madeleine home. When they arrived, Robbie persuaded Chip and Dale to go coach his team for their big game, but only after he promised to keep them informed of Surdas's condition. Mark stayed home with Madeleine, who had suffered more than enough trauma for one day. Aunt Sue and Aunt Allie were sent to Town Hall where the mayoral debate was to be held to await further instruction. Mother, Dad, and Uncles Josh and Mohammed jumped into Dad's car, and arrived at the hospital soon after we did. They were quickly followed by Robbie, who stopped to pick up a tearful Chris, who was blaming himself for not taking Surdas with him to Molly's house.

We all assembled in the waiting room just outside the ER, as the doctors tried to determine what was wrong with Surdas. It is amazing how much of eternity spills into every second you wait for some type of news or assurance that everything is going to be all right. Waiting-room eternities are the longest known to mankind.

Fifty-One

Surdas wasn't exactly sure what happened, but he quickly began to realize something strange was happening now. When he opened his eyes, he was blinded, not by the darkness that he knew so well, but by what must have been light, because it was so different from anything he had ever experienced, that he found it difficult to keep his eyes open.

After a few seconds, it became less difficult, and a voice asked, "Is that better?"

"Yes!" Surdas responded. "But I don't understand what is happening."

"People often have difficulty seeing me in the beginning," the voice responded. "Have no fear. Tell me what you see."

"What?" Surdas asked, dumbfounded at the request. "I am blind and —"

Surdas's response was interrupted by a shape in the light that increasingly became clearer, as the light was drawn into it. Having never seen anything before, he didn't quite know what to make of it. He guessed that it was a young man, perhaps royalty, because his clothes shone as bright as the light that had engulfed him seconds before. Around his neck was a garland of beautiful flowers, and his body appeared to be decorated with many precious jewels. Surdas wondered how he knew what these things were, having never seen them before. But somehow, he did.

In the young man's hair, there was a feather that looked like it had an eye. It was almost as brilliant and beautiful as the eyes of the young man who wore it. Surdas wondered if there could possibly be anyone more beautiful than this stranger, because the very sight of him was so pleasing, that he seemed no stranger at all.

"How is it, that I see all this?" a confused Surdas finally asked, in total amazement.

"Because it is your wish, and my command," the young man answered.

"Are you a genie?"

"More!" the young man laughed, as he raised the flute that Surdas had not noticed in his hand before, and began to play a beautiful tune that brought tears to Surdas's eyes.

"Are you the Lord of my songs and dreams?"

"I am none other," Lord Krishna responded, "because that is how you know me. Others know and see me differently."

"I am not sure I understand, Lord."

"All things are one, My Child. How you see me, is not

as important, as that you see me. It is the message that makes things holy, not the messenger."

"I would say that I see, but I have never seen you, or any other image of The One."

"Still, you know me, do you not?"

"Yes, Lord! Still, I know you. Does this mean that I am dead?"

"It is written that he who remembers me at the hour of death goes to my state of being. So, I ask you, was it me who was in your mind before you arrived at this place?"

"No, Lord." Surdas responded, shyly. "I must admit that it was not. It was Chris."

"Then, My Child, your fate is yet to be determined. Do you know how you came to be here?"

"I remember that I was running."

"Toward your dog or from yourself?" Lord Krishna smiled.

"I'm not really sure what you mean," Surdas responded, thoughtfully. "Yet I guess the answer is yes to both."

"Then you are wiser than you think. But now to the reason you are here. I have come to offer you a choice. It is not an easy one, and it has many ramifications, so choose wisely. If you follow me now, you will see and know all that has been denied you, and more."

"And if I don't?"

"Then you will return to whence you came, and, at least as far as your physical vision is concerned, nothing will change."

As Lord Krishna spoke, the landscape behind him

filled with plants and trees, and creatures of every shape and color. Surdas imagined, that even for sighted people, this would be the most beautiful vision anyone could possibly imagine. He longed to know the names and colors of everything, from the tiniest insect, to the mightiest tree. His brain was soaring with questions, and his heart was soaring with delight. He was truly in heaven, but there was also a catch.

It seems that with every decision in life, even where there is little life in it, there is a catch. And there was everything back on earth attached to this one. Amid all the sights and sounds of the beauty that surrounded him, he was still able to hear voices from the world he left behind. And what he heard, truly broke his heart.

Surdas could hear the sorrow and pain in the voices of his worried family. He heard them crying and praying … Bapu Gene, Bapu John, Chris, everyone. He heard them attempting to bargain with their Creator, offering everything in their power to tempt the Untemptable. He even heard a few of them secretly offering to exchange their lives for his. He heard all this and more. But even more heartbreaking was the fact that he not only heard, but also felt their distress and their love.

"There is so much beauty ahead of you, My Son," Lord Krishna promised, drawing Surdas's attention back to the vision before him. "The majesty before you now is but a small sampling of all that awaits. And yet, there is a different majesty to all you will leave behind. Think carefully before you choose."

"Is that not the case no matter how I choose?" Surdas asked, honestly. "Will the majesty that awaits me, not wait for me, if I wait for it?"

"A wise question with an answer that only you can answer," Lord Krishna smiled. "However, if you follow me now there will be no need for questions and answers. You will see and know all that is, and more. If you return, as I have warned, all will be as before, and you will see no more."

"It is hard to leave behind all that you want. But it is even harder to leave behind all that you love," Surdas responded, thoughtfully.

"Such decisions are never easy, and seldom without a cost," Lord Krishna advised.

"But did I not come into the world for a purpose?"

"Of course!"

"But I haven't fulfilled any purpose, as far as I know. I must still have much to do, because I feel I haven't done much at all."

"Then is not your decision made easier? And if it is not yet your time, why do you think you are here now?"

Surdas seemed somewhat troubled by the question, so Lord Krishna pressed further. "Answer a further question for me. You said it was Chris who was on your mind when you arrived at this place. Were you peaceful or upset at the time he was on your mind?"

"I was upset that he left me to be with someone else," Surdas responded, shyly.

"Why?"

"Because I wanted him to be with me, but he wanted to be with her."

"Which means?"

"It means he loves her more."

"The colors, shapes and forms of love, My Son, are as vast and as beautiful as the universe itself. No love can be weighed or judged in comparison to another. Like the stars, they each have their own value, their own light. Perhaps your purpose will be found in the understanding of this universe."

"I'm not sure I understand," Surdas responded, honestly.

"Yet, My Son, yet! Your understanding, like the decision before you now, will come with a cost. You can choose your destiny, but the purpose of this life expression does not go away. There is an obligation to yourself, that eventually must be fulfilled. If you understand that you have a purpose, then you must give purpose to it.

"For now, that is all you need know. Our time here is coming to an end, and you have a choice to make. Few who arrive here, have this opportunity. You can stay and enjoy all the beauty that surrounds you, or return and try to discover a beauty of your own, and an answer to all the questions that now haunt you."

"When I return, can I at least bring the memory of the colors and shapes you have shown me?"

Lord Krishna laughed, "You have chosen well, Little One. This is not the first time you have given up your sight for a higher purpose. Your namesake did so many centuries ago, when first we met."

"Then we are the same?" Surdas asked.

"Ultimately, we are all the same, My Child. In truth, there are no degrees of separation. We are all one. He who sees the Supreme Lord existing in all beings, truly sees. In this sense, you shall not be blind. But you must be patient; your vision will take time."

"But I have been before?"

"All things have been before, My Child. All things have always been, and will always be, because all things are from the One. Remember all that I have told you, and when the time is right, all will be understood. And, for now, that is enough in the knowing."

"And the memories of the colors and shapes, Lord? May I return with this much of you?"

"I know that you are capable of driving a hard bargain, My Child, so I consider that I'm getting off easy by granting your request," Lord Krishna smiled. "Close your eyes, and listen while I play my flute. When you can no longer hear it clearly, open them again, and you will see me and all that I have shown you no more … save in your mind's eye, where the vision of all that you have seen will remain."

"And You, Lord, will I ever see you again?"

"Of course, My Son! But in the meantime, remember we are never apart. You are my flute, an instrument that brings beauty to the world. When you are true to your higher purpose, you play the most heartfelt music the ear can hear, and the heart can keep a beat to. When you are not, the holes of the flute become blocked, and the world is a much more somber place.

"Now go! Listen to the beauty that we have already composed, and help me play our music in the place from whence you came."

"Then this is goodbye, My Lord," Surdas said, sorrowfully.

"A bye is just an advancement to another round, My Son. It is always good."

Fifty-Two

The years that passed in our first hour outside the emergency room were well worth the wait when the attending physician informed us that Surdas had regained consciousness, and was asking for us. It appeared he had suffered a concussion, but there was no damage to the spine or neck, and a scan of his head appeared normal. The doctor decided to admit him for observation, but he said Surdas would probably be released in the morning.

His doctor said we could spend a little time with him in the ER before they transferred him to a room. He requested that we limit the number of visitors to two at a time. We exceeded the limit by six. Too much of eternity had already passed in the waiting room. We were beyond mortal limitations.

John and I ran to either side of Surdas's bed, grabbed his hands, and kissed his forehead, once again sprinkling him with tears, only this time, tears of joy. We simultaneously whispered, "I love you, Buddy!" and smothered him as gently as possible. Mother, Dad, Robbie, and the uncles patiently waited to follow suit with their affection. Chris still appeared to be traumatized by the situation, and remained at the foot of the bed, just staring at Surdas, and timidly playing with his toes.

Surdas allowed himself to bathe in all the affection before finally speaking.

"Bapu Gene and Bapu John," he began, as he squeezed our hands, "I heard you and everyone else talking to me and praying for me, so I told Lord Krishna that I could not go with him, and came back to be with everyone here. It was so beautiful there. I was almost tempted to stay. But then I realized life with you is even more beautiful. I could not remain there while my heart was here. This is where I belong.

"I wish you could have seen it, though. It was so much better than I could ever have imagined. I saw birds, and creatures, and flowers, and trees, of so many shapes and colors. It was like an amazing dream, only it was real. I can still see it all. I would have come back, even if Lord Krishna didn't let me keep the memories. But He was so kind, that He let me come back with them."

"It sounds quite a bit like the Wizard of Oz, Buddy," Dad suggested. "The important thing is that you are home, right? There's no place like home."

"No! It's important that you understand that it's all real!" Surdas responded, frantically. "It's too real not to be real. I now know these colors, these creatures, and these flowers. I still see them clearly in my mind's eye. You believe me, don't you, Bapu Gene and Bapu John?" Surdas implored.

"We would never doubt you, Buddy," I said, sincerely. "You bring too much certainty to our hearts for our brains not to follow suit. We believe in you, so of course we believe you."

"We all believe you," Mother chipped in, giving Dad a stern look.

"I didn't doubt you, My Boy," Dad apologized. "I only meant that your experience sounded as magical, and as important to you, as Dorothy's adventure was to her."

"Oh! It was … only more so!" Surdas exclaimed, excitedly. "Because unlike her, I actually saw things for the first time in my life. I saw colors, and shapes, and creatures, and what their movements looked like on land, in the air, and on and in the water. I know what they look like, not just what they feel like. And if Chris will stop being afraid, and quit playing with my toes, I'll tell him how well he has described them to me."

"I wasn't playing with your toes," Chris responded, with a half-smile. "I was just making sure you still had eleven."

"Nice try!" Surdas smiled. "If I had eleven, you'd be able to count past twenty."

Chris stepped up to the head of the hospital bed, and gave Surdas a warm hug. And with his head resting on Surdas's chest he asked, "How did you know it was me playing with your toes?"

"I will always know you," Surdas smiled. "I know you as well as I know myself."

"You really scared me," Chris confessed, as his tears began to moisten Surdas's hospital gown.

"How many times have I said that to you?" Surdas laughed, as he wrapped his arms around his buddy and said, "You're trying to drown me again, aren't you?"

"Well don't expect a quick rescue," Chris cried, as the tears continued to flow.

In the midst of all the missed affection, Robbie stepped outside to assure the staff that we would only be violating the rules a little while longer, and to call the rest of the family to update them on Surdas's condition.

He also decided he was exactly where he needed to be at the time. So he called Aunt Sue, who he knew would be waiting for him with Aunt Allie at Town Hall. The debate with the mayor was only minutes from starting. Robbie asked Aunt Sue to inform the mayor that there was no debate as to where he could do the most good. He sent an apology to the audience, but no regrets. He had none.

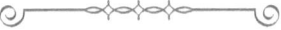

Fifty-Three

Aunt Sue and Aunt Allie were waiting at Town Hall when Robbie's call arrived. Surdas's condition was no longer serious, but Robbie was serious that he needed to be with the rest of the family. He never travels anywhere without his heart, and that's where his heart was. He would miss the debate, but he wouldn't miss missing it. He was staying where he felt he was most needed, or at least where he most needed to be. He would survive the loss that was no longer important to him.

Aunt Sue advised the mayor of the circumstances surrounding Robbie's decision, and relayed Robbie's apologies to all involved. He was about to leave the hall, when he heard the mayor take to the stage with the following announcement:

"Ladies and gentlemen, it appears that my opponent has thought it better not to face me in the debate tonight. That's a shame. You deserve to decide for yourself which one of us would be the better candidate to run this fair town of ours, and I looked forward to demonstrating to you why I have been, and continue to be, that candidate.

"And even though the need for such a demonstration is increasingly becoming less obvious, if you allow me, I will at least uphold my end of the obligation to you, the constituency we are supposed to serve, and press the case a bit further."

The audience could feel the room charge with electricity, as Aunt Sue swung around to face the stage. "I believe it was Confucius who said, 'A man who has committed a mistake, and doesn't correct it, is committing another mistake,'" Aunt Sue raged. "I better hear a correction, Mr. Mayor."

"I don't know what you are referring to," the mayor lied. "Perhaps we can get on with the purpose of this meeting, and let security handle this intrusion."

"Another mistake, Mr. Mayor!" Aunt Sue glared, as he stormed from the back of the room, and took the stage, with two security guards in tow. "You know, you just proved that a mayor, who is his own spokesperson, has a fool for a client."

The mayor made a gesture with his finger, and instructed the guards, "Remove this intruder."

"Are you joking, or are you just the joke? Wave that finger one more time, and I guarantee you, you will be the one wearing these two goons of yours," Aunt Sue sneered, as he easily shook the guards off.

"Apparently, you neglected to inform the audience, that your opponent, Mr. Robbie Poole-Hall, is tending to a family emergency, involving the near fatality of his young nephew. He cannot be here, because family is far more important to him, than demonstrating the very self-evident fact, that he is morally and ethically more qualified for the position he is seeking, than any of his opponents. Or should I say opponent, if we count only one of your faces."

"Now see here," the mayor objected, "I'm only doing —"

"You don't have to explain what you're doing," Aunt Sue interrupted, "unless you have to explain what you're doing. And if you must explain what you're doing, then you're not really doing what you should be doing."

"I believe this person is well out of line, and should be removed from the stage," the mayor demanded, turning toward a rather confused moderator. "Please instruct him, or her, or whatever this person is, to remove itself from the stage."

"Aren't you just the assault of the earth and a slight for sore eyes, Mr. Mayor?" Aunt Sue scoffed. "I really don't care which pronoun you use, as long as it's at least one gender specific. The last person who used one that wasn't, rest his soul, was the last person to use one that wasn't."

'Now look here," the mayor protested, "I'm simply trying —"

"Yes, you are, Your Honor," Aunt Sue interrupted. "You're very trying. And I believe, as your opponent's campaign manager, I have the right to take his place on the stage during an emergency, and explain just how trying you can be."

And then turning to address the moderator, Aunt Sue

added, "You can look it up in the rule book, and see that I am correct, Mr. Moderator, after you leave the stage. You can leave now; we won't need a moderator tonight. I can pretty much guarantee you, there will be no moderation on this stage tonight."

The mayor's smirk completely disappeared, as Aunt Sue redirected his comments once again, "Unless you have something to hide or fear, Mr. Mayor, I suggest we begin."

The mayor's face reddened, and he turned and faced the audience, waving his arms in angered exasperation. "I think the very fact that this person represents my opponent, speaks to the type of moral degradation that we face by his candidacy. I'm all for 'live and let live' within reason. But once we open our public institutions to, anything goes, anything goes will be in our classrooms and places of worship. We're not exactly speaking about family values here, are we folks?"

"Is that what you think, Mr. Mayor?" Aunt Sue replied, as he locked on target. "I think you have another think coming."

Apparently, the mayor never heard Aunt Sue's rule, about always coming to a shoot-out packing. He was about to have a bad hear day.

"There is a lot more venom in your tongue tonight, Mr. Mayor, than there was a few weeks ago at the gentlemen's club, when you tried to put your tongue in my ear."

"That's a preposterous, slanderous lie," the mayor protested.

"I guess that you don't take your memory with you

when you go jogging, Your Honor. So let me jog it for you. I was wearing a short sexy red slice of heaven, and you were wearing some old silk jogging suit that looked like it still had the silkworms attached to it."

"I repeat ... this is absolutely preposterous. I should sue you for that slanderous lie," the mayor interrupted.

"Oh no, Mr. Mayor, you're the one who's about to get Sued," Aunt Sue smiled as he opened his handbag, and handed the mayor an envelope of photos. "The camera is not a politician, Baby. Therefore, unlike you, the camera does not lie.

"You should know, you should never allow the person you're putting the make on, to take compromising pictures, no matter how drunk or high you get. That's the thing that's preposterous. Some of the pictures my friend Allie took are worth a hundred thousand words, so we'll let them do most of the talking. By the way, I had Allie make some extra copies for you to share among your friends and colleagues. They'll be at the press table in the back."

The mayor stood there red-faced and dumbfounded as Aunt Sue continued, "Now, I'm the first to admit that things can get complicated when you mix your drugs. Perhaps you didn't know that all the girls at the 'Girls, Girls, Girls' club, are not all girls, girls, girls. Perhaps you didn't realize that the sexy black femme fatale in the corner was me, your career fatale. And perhaps you didn't realize that there was a little more than your mettle showing, when my friend, Allie, was innocently taking some of those pictures. You could have been confused. That may have been the wrong kind of coke you were mixing with your rum, or perhaps there was some sort of meth to your madness.

"Then again, you weren't too confused to give me that private number. I have it right here in my bag, in your handwriting. And, since every picture tells a story, as you will find in that envelope, I have quite a collection of stories to go with it."

"This is absurd! I'm done here," the mayor ranted, as he stumbled off the stage.

"Oh! You're done all over, Baby. You were done when you tried to fire the first shot. You should never have drawn first. I wasn't looking for this shoot-out. Unlike your 'live and let live' policy, my 'live and let live' policy, actually allows people to live and let live. I didn't plan any of this. I thought that you were just another wolf in cheap clothing when we first met.

"I was perfectly willing to keep my silence about our kismet meeting, and let my nephew, Robbie, figuratively whip your ass, the way you literally wanted me to whip yours in the motel room that night. But, once again, you couldn't wait to discharge your weapon. And, once again, your weapon appears to have jammed up on you.

"Oh, by the way, Baby! In case you're wondering where I disappeared to, soon after we got to that motel room … that something comfortable that I told you I was going to slip into … was a taxi."

As the mayor stormed out of the building, fuming in silence, Aunt Sue fired his last shot.

"Ready, aim, fired, Your Honor! Crappy Diem! Remember, it's better to have loved and lost, than never to have lost at all. And be sure to say 'Hello,' to that lovely wife of yours, who you referred to as, 'the old brawl and chain,' Mr. Family Values. Oh! I'm sorry; excuse my informality; make that, Mayor Family Values."

Queen takes king! Checkmate! Game over!

Fifty-Four

The next afternoon, as Robbie, Chip, and Dale were basking in the glow of Robbie's football team's soccer-score-like 3 - 0 win, and Mother, John, and I were arriving at the hospital to bring Surdas home, it suddenly dawned on me I hadn't given the hospital admitting office any type of personal or insurance information. I mentioned to John and Mother that I should make a quick stop to correct the oversight, when Mother nervously laughed, "You don't think they would have let Surdas be admitted, or leave the hospital, if that wasn't all taken care of, do you?"

"But how?" I asked. "Wouldn't either John or I have to provide all the information, and sign for it?"

"Technically, you sort of, did," Mother replied, sheepishly.

"What?"

"You're my baby. I know everything about you, from your date of birth, to your Social Security number, and any other date or number that they could need. Hell, I could tell them the date of your first wet dream."

"Really? Tell me," John laughed.

"Whoa! Whoa! Too much info," I protested. "But didn't they need my insurance card?"

"And your driver's license," Mother offered. "I gave it to them while you boys were trying to find out information about Surdas."

"But they were in my wallet."

"Were, is the operative word, Sweetie. And after all the innocuous stuff was taken care of, they were safely back again."

"But how …?"

"Let's just say, starving waitresses and drag queens know a thing or two, that no one else needs to know. Every Memory Lane has a few dark alleys."

"And the necessary signatures?" I smiled, quizzically.

"Technically, they were all, sort of, taken care of too. I mean, you were still so occupied, and that childlike font of yours is so easy to copy. I was really trying to help, by making it easier for you boys, with so much going on so quickly.

You and John wanted so badly for this child to be yours. You were both so lost in the moment. I just wanted to make it easier for you. I wanted to make up for not recognizing the hurt I was causing sooner."

"What do you mean?" I asked. "What hurt? You never caused any hurt."

"Yes, I did, Sweetie, not on purpose, but I did. I should

have seen how you felt about Surdas from the beginning. It was the same type of love, longing, and fear I felt when you weren't mine."

"But I've always been yours, at least since I was two."

"Emotionally that's true, Baby, but technically, legally, that didn't happen till much later. There was no such thing as gay adoption when your mom, my sister, passed away. In order to ensure that we could take care of you, she married Dad a few months before she died, so that he could adopt you. Dad became your parent, your legal guardian. But, legally I was left on the outside, looking in. I had no rights, and no recourse for keeping you, if anything happened to Dad. God forbid, had I lost him, I would have lost you both.

"Can you imagine what it would feel like to be told that your child, the child that you love so much, that you would give your very life for—the child that you fed, and clothed, took care of when he was sick, comforted when he was sad, or scared … is not your child? For years I lived in fear, that I would somehow lose you.

"Even when gay adoptions became legal, they were only single-parent adoptions, since there was no such thing as gay marriage. So, the second person still had no legal standing. Once again, I was legally on the outside of the most important life I knew.

"It wasn't until right before we adopted the twins, that gay couples were allowed a two-parent adoption. Even then, I was afraid my job as a female impersonator would stand in the way of finally becoming your legal parent. So

I quit performing, and waited a few months until I felt safe enough to adopt you as a second parent. Dad and I adopted the twins at the same time, though I made sure your adoption went through first, since you had always been my baby."

"How come you never told me this before?" I asked, quite stunned by the revelation.

"The hardest eleven years of my life, were the eleven years I had to wait to become who I always wanted to be, your father, your legal guardian. I guess I never wanted to visit that emptiness again. So, that's why I apologize for not seeing it sooner in you boys with Surdas. I should have seen you were going through the same type of trauma— the same on-the-outside-looking-in emptiness, in the way you loved Surdas. You were experiencing, and I was reliving, the same pain, and I was too afraid to see it, because it was too painful.

"I'm sorry if I went too far in trying to help, or didn't go far enough in revealing things to you. I could probably pave a highway to hell with my good intentions. Are you upset?"

"If I were upset, it would be at myself, for forgetting that Mother is more than a title with you, and for not remembering every minute of every day, how lucky I am to be able to call you that. I'm probably one of the few people in the world who can say, Mother is the best father anyone could ever have."

"Thank you, Baby," Mother whispered, as tears began

to moisten his eyes. "I've always believed, that a mother's larceny is a blessing."

"Now tell me about that wet dream?" John laughed, as we stepped into Surdas's hospital room.

"What!" Surdas screamed in complete surprise. "Who told you?"

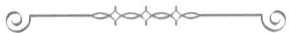

Fifty-Five

The morning after the election, Mother and Dad were having a *My Three Sons* moment, being interviewed by a number of local and national reporters. They were proudly soaring high above cloud nine. We all won our elections: Robbie by a landslide, Chip and I by more than comfortable margins. Now we all had jobs we weren't particularly looking for. But we were more than determined that we weren't going to let anyone down. The difference between us and our opponents, was that we were truly going to try to make one.

The three of us had been extremely gracious and congratulatory in our victory speeches, although the usual concession speeches were noticeably absent. As a matter of fact, neither the mayor, nor his wife, had been seen since the undebatable debate debacle with Aunt Sue. The careers of the mayor and his two cronies had apparently seen bitter days.

Aunt Sue was later quoted as saying, "Asses to asses,

dust to dust … a fool and his monkeys are soon parted. Their greed and prejudices caused their careers to crash—like a couple of lead buffoons."

Fifty-Six

While Robbie, Chip and I were preparing for the changes that were soon to take place in our careers, Surdas and Chris were starting to experience a few changes of their own.

It began slowly, almost imperceptibly, but soon after returning from the hospital, Surdas's demeanor inexplicably began to change. He started becoming withdrawn and sullen, and began spending less time with Chris. He ate less, spent more time alone in his room, and began having difficulty concentrating on his lessons and writing. Strangest of all, he would frequently become belligerent toward some of Chris's invitations, even though Chris amiably kept trying to keep his buddy involved in outside activities, and bring him out of his funk.

John and I were worried that Surdas was still suffering some sort of repercussion from the concussion. But Mother was convinced it was a side effect from the amount of time Chris was spending with Molly during their break from school.

"Surdas really isn't acting very differently from the way you first reacted when Robbie met Mark," Mother reminded me. "We both know how difficult it is, feeling like the odd man out. He needs to find his way back in. He's a little boy, being crushed by a crush. He needs to literally and figuratively see things straight, when it comes to his relationship with Chris."

In any case, we were all worried about Surdas. John and I were putting on our brand-new parenting caps, and planning some sort of intervention, when Mother inadvertently walked in on one of Chris's invitations for Surdas to join him and Molly at the movies.

"It's a date," Surdas replied to the invitation rather rudely. "Do you even know what a date is? It usually involves two people, not a crowd. Do you know how many people make a crowd on a date? Me! I do. I make a crowd. No wonder you never get laid."

"OK!" Chris answered, rather surprised and hurt. "Just asking. I guess I'll see you later."

"Not if I see you first," Surdas muttered, so that only he and Mother could hear. "Like that's ever going to happen."

"Looks like someone is going to have one of my famous talks he didn't ask for, Sweetie," Mother said to a shocked Surdas, who wasn't aware of his presence.

"I was just going to —"

"Have a seat," Mother interrupted sternly. "You were just going to have a seat. You were extremely rude to Chris just now. Actually, you've been pretty rude, and in a pretty foul mood, for quite a while. And there is nothing pretty about it. Whether you realize it or not, your attitude has been affecting the entire family. The rudeness may be directed at Chris, but the moodiness and resentment that accompanies it, affects us all.

"It's time you realized you are part of a family, Baby. Being in a family, is kinda like being in a pool. If you piss in the pool, everyone in the pool has to go through it, at some point. It's not a pleasant experience. And the trouble is, you've been pissed off a lot lately.

"I'm not sure you understand, just how much you've been looking for trouble. But the trouble with looking for trouble, is that eventually you're going to find what you're looking for. And the worst part of finding it, is that the person who is trying the hardest to keep you out of trouble, is the person who you are hurting the most. So, it's probably time we talk about your feelings for Chris, while he still has feelings for you."

"His feelings are for Molly," Surdas whimpered. "She's kind of like the main dish, and I'm kind of like leftovers."

"Yes! He has strong feelings for Molly. They're a beautiful part of who he is. He has every right to them. He wouldn't be Chris without them. And he had those feelings long before you came into his life.

"He also has very strong feelings for you. You know that. As far as I know, he has never demonstrated anything but that to you. That's also a beautiful part of who he is. That's why you feel the way you do about him. That's why you're hurting. And that's why we need to have this conversation.

"I know that your Bapu Gene has discussed the difference in Chris's feelings for you and Molly before, but I think that we have to go over them again, because something isn't getting through to you."

"I know the difference, Mother," Surdas said, sadly as tears started to swell in his eyes. "But knowing, doesn't stop it from hurting. You probably think it's silly but —"

"The problem isn't that it's silly, Sweetie," Mother gently interrupted. "The problem is that it isn't. By not accepting what is real for yourself, you have created an unreal predicament for everyone else. You're making everyone else suffer, because you feel like you're suffering. And I must tell you, Baby, you're the cause of your own pain. You're destroying something absolutely beautiful that you have, because you're upset about something else that you can't."

"I know everything you're saying is true, Mother," Surdas cried. "And I'm sorry. I really am. I don't want to be a problem to anyone, and I don't mean to sound sorry for myself. But I feel so alone when I'm not with Chris. He's like this part of me that wasn't there before ... that makes me better, and whole, and that I never want to lose.

"I know it's not fair to him or Molly, but it's like he's part of something else when he's with Molly, and I'm back on the outside, feeling alone and lonely. The more time he spends with her, the more I feel like I'm losing him. I'm so scared of losing him. Sometimes, I think it's the beginning of the end."

"If you're smart, Sweetie," Mother said, softly, "and I know you're smart, you'll realize that it's not the beginning of the end, it's merely the end of the beginning. All of life is change, and the secret to life, is learning to change with it. The amazing thing about the secret, though, is that the more things change, and the more you change with them, the more they remain the same, even though they may, at times, appear or feel different.

"You're never losing, and you're never on the outside, when you're in someone's heart. It's time you realized, you already are where you need to be. You only need to change the way you're thinking, to remain there.

"You must know how much everyone loves you … especially Chris. The only way you will ever lose him, is to push him away. And whether you realize it or not, that's exactly what you've been doing.

"All relationships go through growing pains. The strong ones help each other grow, even if it means bending a bit to give another the space they need for their growth. Without that growth, the relationship will eventually wither away, and die.

"Let me put it another way. If you take a glass, and smash it on the ground, it's never going to be the same, no matter how often you say you're sorry, and try to put it back together. Relationships are no different. You may try really hard to piece them back together, but once you've smashed them, they no longer hold water, and they're never the same.

"You risk breaking your relationship with Chris, when

you're rude and mean to him. And you risk shattering it even further, when you insult Molly with comments like that 'getting laid' remark. That's dangerously close to breaking the glass, and so out of character, from someone who normally has so much of it.

"Molly has been amazingly considerate of you and your feelings for Chris. You know she loves you too. She unselfishly does everything she can to include you in the time she and Chris have together. Can you imagine how difficult it would be for the three of you, if she put the same type of demands on Chris, that you're trying to do?"

"I know! I know you're right," Surdas responded, tearfully. "I love Molly too. I really do. I know it's not her. She's been nothing but wonderful to me. I know she's not the problem. I know Chris isn't the problem. Neither one of them has ever been the problem. I know that I'm the only problem. And the problem is, I don't know how to stop being the problem."

"You can begin by acknowledging that you've been jealous of the time Chris spends with Molly, and realize just how wrong and unfair it is to everyone.

"Jealousy is a very selfish thing, Sweetie. You can't claim to love the other person more than yourself, if you would steal from their happiness, to enrich your own.

"Both you and Molly are a huge part of Chris's happiness. When you expect more from him than he is capable of being or giving, you steal from that happiness. You rob him of who he is. You destroy a part of that beauty that attracted you to him in the first place.

"Love is a beautifully balanced expression of give-and-take. You can't give more than the other person is capable of receiving, or take more than they're capable of giving, without upsetting the balance, and eventually causing the whole thing to collapse. When you don't allow the other person to be who they truly are, you are taking too much, and giving too little. That is the nature of jealousy; that is what jealousy is all about. And jealousy is a merciless monster, which makes victims of everyone involved, including the person who is jealous.

"It's time to stop being a victim, Baby, and start being a hero. Jealousy is about victims; real love is all about heroes."

"I don't want to be jealous," Surdas wept. "I don't want to be a victim, or make anyone else a victim. But sometimes I am so alone, that it scares me.

"Everything I know, comes from sound and touch. I don't see anything in other people's eyes or expressions. I don't find anything in other people's smiles. Unless the person's feelings are somehow verbally or physically demonstrated, I am always in the dark. I really do try to be brave, and not feel sorry for myself. I'd like to be a hero. But as self-sufficient as I try to act on the outside, it is often not the case on the inside.

"My great-auntie taught me to be a man, while I was still a little boy, in order to protect me. It taught me great survival skills. But I was never really a man, and I missed out on being a boy. Chris taught me how to be a boy again. He showed me the joys of playing, and pretending, and just being who I really was. He laughs when I sound too much like a grown man, and does all sorts of things to bring me back to feeling like a kid again. He makes me feel real, not like someone I have to pretend to be. He makes me feel whole, not like someone lacking something.

"When Chris puts his arm around me to whisper something in my ear, or steers me away from something, or when he tickles me, or wrestles with me, I feel an affection, a happiness, that I never felt in my life. I knew so little of affection and happiness before I came here, and now I want them so much.

"I have to admit, sometimes when I'm not with Chris, I even dream about falling in the lake, just so he can put his arms around me, and rescue me again."

"What lake? What do you mean rescue you again?" Mother asked, worriedly.

"I mean … you know, I dreamt about him rescuing me more than once," Surdas responded quickly, mopping up the secret he had just spilled. "I've dreamt about it a number of times."

"Oh! You scared me, Baby," Mother said, in the panicked breath that Mother Nature included as an intricate ingredient in every mother's nature. "Try dreaming less scary dreams, OK?"

"I'm sorry, Mother! I guess I'm scared, too. I don't know what to do with these feelings. Sometimes it hurts so much. I just want to be with Chris. I want to tell him how I feel, and have him hold me, and tell me it's OK to feel that way. I just want him to hold me. I know I'll never be Molly, but now it's beginning to feel like I'll never be me either. What can I do?"

"It's not simple, and it certainly isn't easy, Baby," Mother began, as he pulled Surdas onto his lap, and squeezed him as tightly as he could. "But you can begin by realizing that you can only love someone for who they are, not who you want them to be. Otherwise, you don't really love that person. You love the fantasy of who that person isn't.

"Real love requires you accept someone as they really are. Place conditions on that person, and you have a contract, not love. The only condition that love asks of you, is that you give and take of it unconditionally.

"Chris loves you the way Uncle Joshie loves me, the way Uncle Robbie loves Bapu Gene. Genie and I had to come to terms with that, or we would have lost great loves in our lives.

"It was perhaps even harder for your Bapu Gene, because he and Uncle Robbie shared the same room, when Gene was experiencing these feelings, and he knew that Uncle Robbie had the same sexual preference. That had to be terribly difficult for him. But he did what he had to do, and came to terms with the reality of the situation, just as I did before him, just as you must do now.

"If we hadn't done that, I probably would have missed my opportunity to meet an even greater love in my life, Dad. And Gene might have missed the great love in his life, Bapu John, which, by the way, still sounds like a cheap Indian pizza joint to me.

"But the point is, the great love in your life, the love

who will love you the way you love him, the way you want and need to be loved, is still out there … somewhere in the not-too-distant future … waiting to find you, the way you're waiting to find him."

"I don't know if I'll ever find another Chris," Surdas said, sadly.

"A brilliant woman named Gracie Allen, who brought joy to the world by pretending to be the opposite, once said, 'Never place a period where God has placed a comma.' That is especially relevant when you're young.

"Life is one long sentence, Sweetie. And the way you live life, is all about the punctuation. Periods become question marks. Question marks become exclamation points. In the end, as you get older, you realize that you have more commas and semicolons than you ever imagined. Do you know what I mean?"

"I think I'm still stuck at the question mark," Surdas responded, sheepishly.

"And that's probably a good thing," Mother smiled. "That's exactly where a ten-year-old should be. The point is, that no matter how certain things seem now, they can change with time. Someday, you'll find someone you love for who they are, not for who they're like. You can easily lose the light of who someone is, if you keep them in someone else's shadow.

"The same will hold true for both Chris and Molly. They're fifteen. They're both very young. What they have now may be a comma or a semicolon. There's too much life left in their sentence to place a period, or even a question mark, anywhere. Just as in your case, the punctuation and tense of their relationship is yet to be determined."

"But it's the question mark that I'm afraid of," Surdas responded, sadly. "I can't imagine my life without Chris."

"Chances are, you won't have to, if you imagine your life with him correctly," Mother assured him. "He loves you the best way he can. Love him back the best way you can; the way that you know is right for him, for you both. It won't be simple. It won't be easy. But you'll never regret it, and the rewards are far greater than you can possibly imagine.

"In the meantime, I'll try to make sure we all remember that you're more ten-year-old boy than sixteenth-century poet. And I'll see to it that we all keep all the attention, hugs, and kisses you need and deserve coming your way."

"Only when I deserve them," Surdas smiled slightly, as he started to return to his self-confidence.

"You will always deserve them," Mother promised. "And stop worrying about whether you'll ever meet somebody. You're only ten years old for Krishna's sake. You have at least another twenty years before I'm ready to see someone sweep my beautiful dark prince away."

"Oh Lord!" Surdas worried at the mention of Krishna's name. "I am so stupid. I forgot. I have not been very true to my higher purpose. Lord Krishna must be so upset with the holes that I plugged in my flute."

"I'm not really sure what that means, Sweetie," Mother responded, somewhat confused. "But I'm pretty sure He'll get over it, as soon as you get over it."

"Thanks, Mother," Surdas smiled, as he hugged and kissed his mentor. "I love you. I love you all. And I'm sorry for all the trouble I've caused everyone. I guess I owe Chris and everyone a big apology."

"Chris would be the best start," Mother said, as he returned the hug and kiss.

"I'm going to clear the air, and explain everything to him," Surdas said, nervously. "I owe him ... actually I owe us both that much."

"Is there anything I can do to help?" Mother asked, perhaps even more nervous at the prospect of the pending conversation than Surdas.

"Wish me luck," Surdas smiled. "You've already done wonders helping me."

If I've already done wonders, why doesn't this feel more wonderful? Mother asked himself as Surdas left. *I just had an adult conversation with a young boy, who sounds more adult than I ever will; and yet, is, and needs to be, a child more than anyone I've ever known. I wonder which one will have the conversation with Chris.*

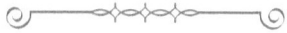

Fifty-Seven

It was not Mother's intention to either question Surdas's quest or respond to Chris's response, but he immediately sought out Robbie, Mark, John, and me after his conversation with Surdas. He thought it better for us all to be prepared for any possible outcome of Surdas's coming out to Chris.

We were all sure that Chris would handle the situation well. It's part of who he is. It seems there are few situations that he doesn't handle well. We just weren't sure if well was good enough, considering Surdas was baring his heart and soul to the object of his desire, for the first time in his young life. Anyone who was ever in that position, knows all too well, that even the gentlest of rebuffs leaves lifelong scars, once the wound has been exposed.

Mother's plan was dinner, of course, at Robbie and Mark's house, so that we would all be there when Chris returned home from his date with Molly. Most of Mother's plans are centered around home-cooked food, the all's fare in love and war.

"Admit it! Doesn't the thought of food usually lead to food for thought?" he would often quip. "That's why heavy thinkers are usually just that."

Mother limited the dinner to Dad, Surdas, both sets of parents, and Madeleine, so as not to draw suspicion of a planned gathering. As usual, the planned gathering fooled no one, but I had the feeling Surdas was thankful for the support and smaller crowd.

We were just finishing the quieter than usual dinner, when Chris returned home from his date. Surdas immediately excused himself from the table, and asked Chris if he could speak to him outside on the porch. As the boys stepped outside, and closed the door, Mother, Dad, Robbie, Mark, John, and I all rushed to every possible crack in the door and windows to hear the conversation. Little Madeleine was left on her own to feed Angel and Hopi everything that was left on the table.

"If you're going to tease me again about not getting laid," Chris began defensively, as they stepped outside, "not that it's any of your business, but that's not what Molly and I are about. She's better than that, and you should be too. Someday, someone is going to teach you that it is more important to let love make you, than it is for you to make love. Until then, maybe you should find some other way to be mean."

"I know," Surdas said with tears in his eyes. "I'm so sorry, Chris! I didn't mean to be mean. I didn't mean any of it.

I didn't mean to smash the glass. I just got scared, because I love you!"

"What? I mean … I know, you little dope, I love you too," Chris confessed, somewhat confused and taken aback. "I don't get it. What's going on? What glass? Why are you scared? And why have you been so mean lately?"

"I guess I got jealous of the way you feel about Molly, and the more I realized it, the more afraid I became of losing you. I didn't know how you'd feel, when you realized that I love you the way you love Molly, not the way you love me. I was afraid that you'd be upset with me, or embarrassed, or something, and wouldn't want anything to do with me anymore."

"What? Are you serious? Get over the thousand and one dumb blond thing, Scheherazade. I've known how you felt for a while."

"You have? Why didn't you tell me?"

"I didn't know it was a secret. I thought we both knew how each other felt, and it was cool."

"So, you're not upset with me because of the way I feel about you? I didn't scare you away? You don't hate me?"

"Now who's the dumb one? Do you honestly think I'd be upset, or love you any less, because you love me differently? Does that make any sense at all? Do you hate me because I love you differently?"

"No! But it did kind of drive me crazy for a while."

"Been there, Bronco," Chris smiled. "We all do our share of crazy around here. Even if, for the most part, we're all unrelated, it's still kind of an extended family trait.

"I think the important thing is, to get past the crazy, snap back, and realize how much we already have, which is a lot, when you stop to think about it. Do you know what I mean? So, are you back, or are you still snapped?"

"I think I'm pretty much back," Surdas began to cry. "I'm so sorry for being mean, and hurting you though. I never wanted to hurt you, or Molly.

"Sometimes, when I knew that you guys were kissing, or I could feel your lips when you were whispering something in my ear, I'd fantasize what it would be like to have a real kiss from someone like you, someone who cares about you, someone you love. I've never had a real kiss before. I guess that's when the crazies set in. The more I thought about it, the crazier I became. I guess my mood eventually became as dark as the night."

"You know the night isn't really ever that dark," Chris smiled. "There are actually millions of stars, little dots of light, that show you the way, while the sun is blocked. Moods are kind of like that. If you look past the darkness, there are all these specks of hope and light, reminding you that the dark is merely a shadow of something blocking the light."

"Wow! That's pretty profound for a blond boy," Surdas sniffled. "That would even be pretty profound for Uncle Joshie.

"I'm so sorry, Chris! I'm sorry that my jealousy blocked your light. You're a star, a real star. You've always been one to me. I'll try never to block your light again, I promise. Can you forgive me?"

"There's nothing to forgive, Buddy," Chris responded, sincerely. "The important thing is that we're out of the shadows and into the light. We're fine!"

"So we're really going to be … OK?" Surdas asked, timidly.

"Sure, stop and think about it," Chris smiled. "We're not exactly alone in any lovefest around here. We've got great teachers … pretty experienced teachers from the stories they've told us. We'd have to really screw things up, to really screw things up. As long as we try to respect and understand each other, there's nothing we can't get through."

Inside the house Robbie gave me a "that's my boy" thumbs up and wink, that we all returned with a "that's our boy" smile.

Outside the house, Surdas was thoroughly relieved, thoroughly shaken, and thoroughly in tears.

"Are you OK, Bronco? Do you need me to hug you?" Chris asked, sincerely with his arms outstretched,

"Yes, Cowboy Chris!" Surdas confessed, as he stepped through the outstretched arms, that he somehow sensed were there, and into the hug that he so desperately needed. As he did so, tears broke out everywhere inside and outside the house. "I'm sorry that I hurt you, and I'm sorry about the whole dumb blond thing," Surdas continued.

"That's OK! I like your jokes," Chris confessed.

"I didn't mean the jokes," Surdas smiled, trying to end the tears. "I just meant that you're blond."

"Now that's the Bronco I know and love," Chris laughed, truly embracing the hug.

Chris continued to hug and comfort Surdas well after the tears subsided, and the rest of the family gave up their spying positions, and returned to dinner cleanup duties. The two boys sat on the porch steps for another hour or so, with Chris's arm around Surdas, talking about friendship, and life, and further adventures, but mostly just enjoying the silence of each other's unspoken friendship and love. It's amazing how many volumes are written when words don't get in the way.

As all the wounds healed, and the two boys stepped back into the house, the radio was playing Aretha Franklin's version of *Nessun Dorma* in the background:

"Within my heart my secret lies, and what his name is none shall know ... No! No!"

As Mother always says, "There are no coincidences." Chris, perhaps sensing the irony, smiled, gave Surdas a hug from behind, and planted a tender kiss on the top of his head. As he did so, Surdas practically melted, and the tears began to well in his eyes again.

"Now what, Bronco?" Chris asked, gently. "Did I do something wrong?"

"No! No! You don't understand! That's my first real kiss," Surdas cried. "I wished all along that it would come from you. And now, my wish has come true. It may sound silly to you, but it is a treasure that I will always remember."

"Dude, I'm sure that your dads and Mother kiss you all the time," Chris responded, rubbing his buddy's head where the kiss still ran warm.

"Yes, but they kiss me the way parents kiss their child," Surdas protested. "That's different. That doesn't count."

"Tell that to them," Chris laughed. "Parents not only count, but they also keep ledgers. Anyway, you're not even eleven. You shouldn't be thinking about these things yet. I'm still teaching you how to be a kid, Romeo."

"I'm sorry!" Surdas whimpered, the tears flowing freely again. "I know I'm being stupid. I don't mean to be. I must be a pretty dumb kid because I don't know what's wrong with me. I dreamed that you kissed me. And now you have. So now I'm happy, but I'm crying. I don't get any of it. It's so stupid! I'm sorry!"

"Don't be! You're my best friend," Chris smiled, as he wiped the tears on Surdas's cheeks.

"I know," Surdas sniffled.

"I love you like a brother."

"I know."

"I would do anything for you."

"I know. I know."

"Anything!" And before Surdas could respond, Chris gently took Surdas's hands, placed them on his eyes so that Surdas could also understand the moisture in Chris's eyes, then slowly moved them down to the smile on his face, and tenderly kissed the palms of both hands.

Surdas was astounded by the gesture. He backed away in tearful amazement. As he did so, you could tell by the smirk on Chris's face, that he understood how momentous the occasion was for his buddy, so he decided to seize the moment further, and gently kissed Surdas's cheek and lips.

"I don't understand," Surdas whispered. "You kissed me. You kissed me the way I kissed you, and then kissed me even better."

"I know," Chris smiled.

"But you're not even gay. You're straight."

"I'm pretty sure that I know that too," Chris smiled. "Why does a kiss have to be gay or straight? Maybe it's just something between us, right now, a Cowboy and Bronco thing. Maybe it's just my way of telling you how much you mean to me ... how much you'll always mean to me."

Surdas looked confused. It was an act of love and compassion beyond anything he had ever imagined. He couldn't respond. He didn't know what else to say.

"I can't be the man of your dreams, Bronco," Chris continued, gently rubbing his best friend's head, "but I'll always do anything I can, to help make your dreams come true. That much I can do. As much as I can, I will.

"Someday, when you're much older, the man of your dreams will kiss you in a way that will take your breath away. But even after that, I will love you, and be there for you." And then, placing Surdas's hand on his heart, and his hand on Surdas's, he continued, "We are always here, Bronco ... in all ways, always!"

As the understanding of the gesture slowly made its way to Surdas's consciousness, the tears that had been welling in his eyes turned to pools of joy, and he beamed the brightest smile I have ever seen. After a few more perplexing seconds, he slipped back into Chris's embrace with a solemn vow.

"I know you kissed me to make my dream come true, Chris. And I will always love you for that, and for everything else you do. In ways that even I do not understand, I think that you have saved me again.

"Once again, you are my hero. You are always my hero. Your gift, the kisses, will always be our secret. You needn't worry. No one will ever know, not even Bapu Gene and Bapu John. This is forever just between us. I promise!"

"That's going to be a hard promise to keep, Little Brother," Chris laughed, putting Surdas's hand to his lips, so that he would understand the smile. "Half the family, including your parents and mine, are standing on the other side of the room, grinning at us. And I can guarantee you, that the other half, especially Chip and Dale, will know everything before the night is over."

"Oh, no, Chris! I'm so sorry," Surdas cried, in shock. "I didn't mean to embarrass you. I'm such a little wuss. I embarrassed us both."

"You didn't embarrass anyone," Chris assured him, as Mother whispered how much he loved Surdas's little wuss, in the background. "It's not like I didn't know they were here. They're all quiet, and there isn't a dry eye in the house, so you know they didn't find it embarrassing. How often does the quiet part happen in this family? Besides, these guys kiss each other all the time."

"Sorry guys!" I chimed in. "Don't let our presence take anything away from the presents you just gave each other. We're all so proud of you both, and we're all deeply touched and honored to have been here."

"One more thing!" Chris added. "Because it was you, I have to admit the kisses felt kinda cool. It may not be the kinda cool that I'll blast all over the internet, but I have no problem with anyone in the world knowing that my first real same-sex kiss was with the best friend I've ever had. The only problem I have is with anyone who has a problem with that."

Robbie high-fived me, as we, and the rest of the family, surrounded our sons in one gleeful loving hug. The absolute beauty and understanding that Chris brought to the situation was breathtaking, and had us all in tears. As the embrace slowly broke, and Surdas finally left his best friend's arms, Mother pulled him aside, and whispered to him, "Congratulations, Sweetie! I'm sure Krishna's very proud of you. And, between you and me, I think you had better adjust yourself; it looks like your little flute has become unplugged."

The joyous group headed back to the table, unplugged flute adjusted, just as the phone began to ring. It was the former mayor of New York City. He called to offer Robbie his congratulations on the election, and inform him that he intended to run for governor next year. "I'm going to need a young dynamic running mate," the older man offered. "My team and I think you're that man. Don't answer right away. Think about it! This is a golden opportunity. There are millions more kids out there that you may eventually reach. You can really make a difference. You never know where something like this can lead. Talk it over with your family, and let me know what you think."

As a stunned Robbie hung up the phone, he looked around the room at the texting orgy already being sent out by the excited eavesdroppers. It appeared they were already making up his mind. He knew there was a large "Curve Ahead" sign written in the smiling eyes of every one of his family members, and he started to think that he had better learn to bend with it.

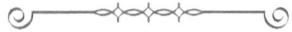

Conclusion

In many ways, Surdas had thrown Chris a not-so-normal curve. It wasn't the first curve in Chris's young life, so he knew how to handle it. But he didn't just bend with it. He stepped up to the plate and hit it out of the park … just as Robbie was preparing to do … just as we all should do. Chris didn't question the pitch. He knew better. Love should never be questioned … only answered.

About the Author

Over the past thirteen years, Stephen J. Mulrooney has honed his skills of writing and has now become an accomplished author. His previous two novels in this series of *NORMAL?*, have achieved critical acclaim, such as his True Colorz Honor Role selection. Steve's thirty-something year dream of becoming a writer began to take shape in 2009 when the characters in these books began telling him their stories. It took another three years before he realized the best way to become a writer was to actually sit down and write. It helped.

NORMAL TOO? was Steve's second book and the much-anticipated sequel to its predecessor. Apparently, the characters that told Steve their story in the first book haven't stopped talking. He hopes you enjoyed their further adventures in that book as much as he has.

NORMAL CURVE? is Steve's much awaited third novel in what Steve has decided to extend into a series. It has been ten years since Steve finished the first draft of *NORMAL CURVE?*. During most of that time, it sat patiently waiting for our return to it, to cut and polish it into the beautiful gem it has become.

Steve still lives in Kansas City, MO, with his husband, Jerome P. Van Wert, and their, now, feline family. In the past ten years, their many rescue dogs have gone over the rainbow bridge. Tigger, the incredible cat, showed up one day and eventually took up residence.

Stephen J. Mulrooney

Busterfly

Why did I name the company Busterfly?

Our Friend's Story

The name Busterfly is a tribute to our wonderful canine friend, Buster. Buster was a male Neapolitan Mastiff. He came into our lives one cold February evening. If you would like to read the full story, or if you would like to stay up to date with Stephen J. Mulrooney's continued adventures with the NORMAL? series, or meet up with Steve for a book signing, check in every-so-often at the link below.

www.busterfly.com

LOOK FORWARD TO STEPHEN J. MULROONEY'S
NEXT BOOK IN HIS NORMAL? SERIES

NORMAL VISION?

STEPHEN J. MULROONEY

Busterfly
Kansas City, Missouri

www.ingramcontent.com/pod-product-compliance
Lightning Source LLC
Chambersburg PA
CBHW020949260626
47169CB00006B/1892